Sane Asylum

Sane Asylum

Allison Whittenberg

Apprentice House Press
Loyola University Maryland

Copyright © 2023 by Allison Whittenberg

All rights reserved. No part of this book may be reproduced or transmitted in any form or by any means, electronic or mechanical, including photocopy, recording, or any information storage and retrieval system, without prior permission from the publisher (except by reviewers who may quote brief passages).

First Edition

Library of Congress Control Number: 2022950401

Hardcover ISBN: 978-1-62720-454-5
Paperback ISBN: 978-1-62720-457-6
Ebook ISBN: 978-1-62720-458-3

Design by Brian Leechow
Editorial Development by Corrine Moulds

Published by Apprentice House Press

Loyola University Maryland
4501 N. Charles Street, Baltimore, MD 21210
410.617.5265
www.ApprenticeHouse.com
info@ApprenticeHouse.com

To veterans

One

His skin, under the bandages, itched like a mother. It was still the middle of the night. Three or maybe four in the morning. It was so dialed down in the ward. All Coop could hear was a hum.

How long had he been in here? How many days? It's so difficult to keep the clockwork straight.

The small of his back was sore. Coop arched and heard a crack. What was he all of a sudden, seventy?

How easy it had been to get like this—tormented by his immobility, his helplessness.

How long had he been in here? He had lost track of the days. It was cold, and it was so dark. It was very quiet.

Coop squirmed in the bed and gave the territory just above his ass a good scratching and, for a second, felt relieved. Then it was back to his eyes. The bandages were beyond irritating. They burned.

He had two choices: go back to sleep or press the button.

If Coop tapped out for assistance, they'd give him more of that shit. It would give him that dizzy sensation.

That shapeless feeling.

Did he beyond doubt want to get that loopy again? That grainy?

There was a third possibility; he could nod off and

imagine that nurses would appear and instead of drugging him, he could get attended to with the new strips and pads like that. They would change his sheets and fluff his pillow in his imagination. They'd imaginarily massage his temples.

Dreams are sweet. They made him feel cool, as if blamed for the war. Dreams are like drugs, addictive. Pretty soon you lose track of what the facts are.

His index finger hovered over the pager, without pressing it.

All the earlier noises—the voices, the clanging, banging, voices and rustling had subsided. With all this abundant quiet, what was there to fear?

He is a soldier.

He was a soldier.

"You can make it. You can take it," the drill instructor said during those simulated death marches at Fort Hood where Coop trained.

They humped hills, rucksacks hitched high on their backs.

Things were simple back then, real Disney World. The training he received was theoretical. There was hour after hour of instruction and Coop never wondered to what end.

He was eighteen back then. Eighteen and energetic, not idealistic but boundless in energy.

What time was it? How soon till dawn?

Silence persisted, yet there was a drumming in his ear.

And under the bandages, he was blind.

That last part wasn't for certain. That's what this whole dog and pony show was about. It was a big wait and see—literally.

Wait and see if he could see.

Coop cracked a smile. He always appreciated irony.

Could I make this? Could I take this? He asked himself, and sighed, as he shook his head from side to side; *I should have never knocked on her door...*

Two

But back then, there were so many doors to open. And that was Coop's mission as an MP. From the early morning hours to late in the evening, he opened door after door, and got at what was behind them.

Coop worked with another guy called Johns. Tony Johns. Johns was a talker, a yakker. Shorter than him, with quick green eyes, Johns was about Coop's age. He was from one of the New York boroughs, so his wordiness came out fast. As they rode up to the Northeast suburb of a Philadelphian cul-de-sac that housed the fifth name on the list they were working on that day, Johns not only started conversations, but he worked mightily to keep it going.

"I mean it was no <u>Death of a Fucking Salesman</u>, but it was still deep as shit," Johns said.

"And it's called <u>The Dungeons of Doom</u>?" Coop asked. "Don't let that throw you. They may have gotten that part wrong but the rest of it was deep, and I do mean deep."

"I get it. I get it," Coop said agreeing just for the sake of agreement, thinking that would suffice Johns and they could move on to something else.

Like a dog with a bone, Johns continued gnawing about the movie he'd seen. "Sometimes the simplest of ideas have the most layers underneath. That's what makes a simple story so complex."

Coop parked at the head of the street. "I don't know, Johns. I'm always leery of any of those straight-to-DVD DVDs."

"But don't you see," Johns said, "the zombies were a stand in for Al Qaeda."

Coop shook his head as they approached the house, which was a red brick with vanilla siding. Their heavy boots stepped lightly on the quiet of the cement sidewalk.

Coop clucked his tongue. "I don't like zombies." Johns stood next to Coop. "You don't like zombies? Who doesn't like zombies?" Johns asked in a nasal fast voice.

"I don't," Coop said as he double checked the name with the place.

"How could you not like zombies?" Johns asked.

They walked past the house and hovered to the side of it.

"How could you not like zombies?" Johns repeated.

"That's like un-American."

"I thought you said they represented Al Qaeda?" Coop asked as he folded the sheet with the names and house numbers his superiors gave him. He stuck it back in his case.

Coop blanked out during the explanation that Johns gave him and talked over him saying, "I don't understand the zombie rules."

"How do you even kill a zombie? Sometimes it seems if they fall over with a good wind, other times they are shot repeatedly, and they still keep coming."

Johns went on to explain the sci-fi-technobabble of zombie lore as Coop worked up for the next step. The street was quiet during this mid-day.

"Most importantly if a zombie bites you, you don't have to turn into a zombie. Some humans are naturally resistant to zombies."

Coop shook his head. "Well, that's not me. If there's a virus anywhere, I'll get it."

Johns made this joke: "I have a computer like that."

Coop almost did a 'ba-dum-ba' drum imitation but changed his mind. Things had gotten like that. He couldn't even complete a joke because everything felt too heavy. He envied Johns frenzied but loosey goosey attitude. Nothing seemed to get to him.

Coop scraped his foot across the gravel.

"At least, it had the guts to call them out. Most big budget flicks would never do that," Johns said.

Coop sighed. Now things were taking a turn. He could predict what Johns would say next.

"I'll tell you one thing," Johns began, his voice taking on an air of righteous indignation. "If I was a half Scotland and half Italian who rammed a plane into a skyscraper and killed 3,000 people, I would expect to be called something."

Coop held up his hand. "Johns, I don't want to get into politics."

"Then what the Hell did you sign up for?"

Coop did basic training back in his home state, two dozen states away from where the terrorist struck. From what Coop gathered, Johns, coming from the heart of things, was the rarity. Most of the recruits he'd met in basic were from wide open spaces like Montana and Maine.

Coop for a moment tried to remember what his uniform felt like the first time. When his fatigues were crisp and with the scent of a factory... When his boots were brand new with the smell of leather... Now, it was something he put on and off, like a costume.

"Hating the enemy is the only fun of war," Johns said. "I mean what the fuck else is there to look forward to when you're shipped 5,000 miles from home, the MREs?"

Coop laughed, in spite of himself. Rarely did he really stop to think about things, and when he did, he realized he was on that razor's edge between comedy and tragedy, tipping ever so slightly toward the funny.

The next part Johns said required no laugh track. "Do you even know what the enemy looks like?"

Now Coop frowned. "You do, Johns?"

"I do."

"How could you? They could be anywhere. They could be anyone. They don't have to be Al Qaeda."

"They could be Al Qaeda. They could be hippies."

"Hippies?"

"I know what the enemy looks like. It looks like confusion. And chaos. It's the damnedest thing: everybody wants to be American, but nobody wants to be an American. This is a crisis. We shouldn't have to knock on doors. We need all hands-on deck. I'd like to tell these people that they are Americans whether they like it or not. They can root for the enemy all they want but when is said and done: If America falls, they fall. Those motherfucking warmed over leftover freeze-dried hippies can put that in their peace pipe and smoke it."

Coop let Johns' words snap and crackle, but he didn't answer him. How could he? What could he say besides maybe he didn't know Johns as well as he thought he did.

They stood on the narrow landing, and Coop knocked on the door.

"Mrs. Winslow, we're here about Nathan Winslow, your son." No reply.

Coop exchanged a look with Johns.

There was a peephole. Coop couldn't help but wish it pointed the other direction, if only he could press his pupil to the hole. But it didn't work like that; it only pitched toward the street.

Inside, footsteps moved. Coop heard them, heavy and deliberate. Slow about the doorway. Then they went faint.

"What the fuck is taking so long?" Johns asked.

Coop shrugged his shoulders.

The sky was so blue and clear. They were the sole noise on the street as the soldiers knocked again. A drop of sweat slipped down Coop's back. He rolled back his shoulders to relax.

"Open up, ma'am, we know you're in there. We're here on behalf of the government of the United States," Johns said. Again, no reply.

Coop didn't grow up curious. There wasn't a whole lot he wanted to know. This wasn't what he figured he was getting into. He thought MPs would be protecting people during national emergency or martial law, maybe a little crowd control, but he never wanted this door-to-door shit.

"Come on, come on. What's taking so long? Roll out of bed, slap your girdle on, and open the door." Johns pounded on the door.

Quiet. So very quiet, like duck fat rolling a roasting pan. What was the wait about?

They stood outside and Coop got a sinking feeling that

that dusty old notion of patriotism wouldn't work this time. But this was all part of a day's work, this steering into the skids.

"Let's move on," Coop said.

Johns shook his head. "No, someone's in there."

Coop looked away from the door and back to the car. They were only a few paces away. Maybe everything was still normal like the Quaker Oats he had for breakfast that morning. Or was it Cream of Wheat?

"Let's move on," Coop insisted.

Johns didn't budge. "They got all this, and they still aren't grateful."

Johns rapped on the door again and continued, "They get the most out of this country. Put these people on the front line."

"Are you sure they have the heart?" Coop asked.

Johns kicked at the door and said, "They'll grow a heart."

Coop stilled Johns.

Johns resisted and said, "Come on, Lady. We're here about your son. His ship date was-"

Just then, the door punched open. She blind-sided them, this mother, hitting the rail like a bullet. She wielded a meat cleaver. Her arm went hacking and slicing. Such force, spinning in different directions. She had a ridiculous aim, and she foamed like white water. Her arms were bare and very thick, especially her upper arms which displayed like meaty hammocks. The blade came at them strong. Writhing and twisting.

Pop eyed with surprise, Johns was slow to react at first. Coop took swift action but she outweighed him by a good seventy pounds. Still, the clumsy, uncoordinated hand-to-hand maneuver of two men in their twenties should have taken down a fifty plus woman easily. So what if she was a mother? So what if she had a sharp weapon? That cleaver so far hadn't left a mark.

Did people even use them anymore? Wasn't there some butcher to get a half a pound of this or that?

When Coop subdued her, she turned around and started slicing at Johns. When Johns subdued her, she turned around and started slicing at Coop.

"You're not taking him!" she screamed.

They scrambled to get a hold of her. When they finally did, Coop had an empty bleached feeling. What was won? There they were, two grown men pinning down a woman's hands, elbows, and legs.

Coop flipped her over. He took out the cuffs and clipped them on her thick wrists and hoisted her up.

"You can't force my son to go anywhere," she told them.

"Your son is no better than us," Johns said.

"Oh, yes, he is."

Johns picked up the meat cleaver and with one swoop, he stabbed. He cut. He sliced. He hacked.

"Johns!" Coop shouted.

Three

It was customary to give an after-action report at the end of the day.

Coop followed the maze of linoleum to the room that was just off the right corridor, the little room where the brass congregated.

He smelled the floor polish as he walked into the room. He took his assigned seat five spaces away from his staff sergeant, who had big black eyes that stuck out a little permanently, not just when he was excited. He greeted Coop with a short nod.

Coop hadn't even changed from this afternoon. He'd come right from the hospital to here. Everyone else in the room had uniforms so stiff they cracked.

Outside, there was a harangue of protesters. Coop had to shove through them just to pass the main gate. Though they were several yards from the building, their voices carried. They kept saying the same thing: "Down with America."

The platoon leader pulled the blinds down and said, "I think things will get a whole lot worse before they get better."

Coop turned to see a long line of flat expressions from the others in the room. They were about twenty men around that large pinewood table.

An E-7 came in and was saluted. He eyed Coop and said without irony, "Tough day, huh?"

Coop flirted with insubordination by lifting his eyebrows.

"Where was Johns taken to?"

"He's being well taken care of," the E-7 said.

Coop swallowed and thought long and hard before asking the question. "Where?"

No one at the long table answered him.

"Isn't there going to be an investigation? A trial? Where's JAG?" Coop asked.

The staff sergeant rose from his seat and walked over behind Coop's chair. He placed one hand on Coop's shoulder.

"Sergeant Cooper, these are very difficult times, and we must be very careful about what we do in this particular period in history."

Coop twisted around and gave his superiors a look of kinetic confusion. They were all so stiff they seemed perpetually at attention.

His eyes moved to the solitary person in the room he did outrank. A female, a PFC. Kind of thick around the waist and pie faced but she had a nice smile. She was smiling as she keyed in the preceding into her laptop. Coop never understood admin. Why would anyone join the Army to take notes? It's not like there was ever a shortage of secretarial jobs in the civilian world.

The only other woman in the room was an E-5 like Coop. Her name was Ybarra. Ybrarra had stiff bangs and she always seemed rigid to him. Coop always liked her even though she never crossed her legs. At any rate, she was towing the party line, falling in lock step with the other green in the room.

Outside, the protesters kicked up again with their "down with America" drone.

A shiver ran over Coop. The room seemed smaller and the air was stuffy.

The Staff Sergeant bent forward a little. "To some brutality is a put on, others you have to draw it out of them."

"With all due respect," Coop began.

"We're all adults here," the Staff Sergeant said, talking over him. "Let's just cut to the chase."

Coop nodded.

"What every you saw, forget it," he said slowly emphasizing each word.

Was he going to sweep all this under the rug? Was there a rug that big? What was with the smooth over? The buttery NPR tone of calm collected order when in fact there was a need to panic. Why couldn't Coop talk about the feral hate that that mother came at them with? Could he speak on the breaking point that anyone would come to after that? Couldn't the brass leave him with some basic instruction on what do you do when the routine is no longer routine?

"The important thing is that you're alright."

A surge of nausea rose in Coop. "Yes, sir."

"... And you are able to continue the mission."

"Yes-" he began but something was caught in his throat before he could finish.

Four

After the meeting, Coop went outside and leaned against the wall.

"Hey, Coop, Powerball's up to 999 million." Spc Morin said, "That's a lot of power for a ball to have."

"Down with America!" A small disorganized but disgruntled mob shouted.

Morin shook his head as he looked at them from the distance of the smoking section. "No, up with America, you ex-hippies. If I win the Powerball, I'm paying off the national debt."

Morin's glasses slipped off the bridge of his nose as he exhaled the smoke. The ashes fell. To Coop, he said, "Only in America can a draft dodger be elected president and Vietnam vets have to sleep in a cardboard box."

Coop lit up as he listened. From these breaks, smokers know each other. Coop had heard all this before from the fifty something SPC-4 Morin. You have to have worked long and hard to be that old and stifled at that pay grade. The Army tends to like to move people up the chain, especially during times of conflict. Like in Grenada, out of 5000 troops they awarded 800 medals. That's better odds than any lottery. It was always more medals, more fruit salad to go on the class As. Coop figured that Morin's lost prophet persona was the reason he'd been overlooked in promotion time and time again. Worse than failing your PT test or sleeping with the CO's wife was Morin's constant philosophizing—nobody likes a wiseass.

"The fun thing is. This Winslow woman's son probably made it to the Canadian border by now or maybe he's mixed up with this protest shit," Morin said.

Coop frowned and peered out at the thirty or so strong, blue jeaned contingency. He lit up a cigarette.

"I bet he's one of these shaggy string beans out here. That would be one of God's jokes. Instead of defending his country that needs him, he's farting around with these fucked up fucks," Morin said.

"I just can't believe Johns snapped like that. You know Johns, did you see that coming?"

"Who am I to separate the crazy from the soon-to-be crazy?"

"He was fine until she opened the door. The way she acted about her son. She acted like everyone else could go but not her son."

Morin smirked as he eyed the mob. "There's a lot of that going around."

"I just wish I knew what was on the other side of that door."

"Trust me, if you knew ahead of time you wouldn't go in."

"End the war!" A man in a dark blue windbreaker growled.

"Oh, will you shove it already?" Morin yelled back.

"Shove it where?" That man asked.

"Anywhere but here," Morin said.

The man gave Morin the finger (again) and went back

to walking in circles.

There seemed to be a sulfur rotten egg odor in the air all of a sudden as they went back to their threats, their appeals.

"I think some of them really hate us," Coop said.

"Well, that brings tears to my eyes," Morin said, "My pop was a combat medic in 'Nam. Coming back to the states after his first tour at the airport an attendant directed him and the other soldier to back away from the baggage claim and let the paying customers get their luggage first. My old man told me how he watched them one by one breeze past, and he started lapsing. Going back to the way he was pre-war. He started to ask why. Then he stopped himself. He remembered himself. He came back to what he'd become."

"What had he become?" Coop asked.

"Someone who doesn't question."

Coop nodded.

"That's what life is about… It's not about beauty or truth or money or poetry or politics or women. It's not about fairness. It's about getting through each day."

"I know what you mean," PFC Tanenhaus said, he'd been listening from the fray. "I always wanted to be a soldier like my father and my uncle. Experience the lifestyle I had heard so much about. My uncle was just a cook, but my pop went med. The army sent him straight through school. He'd been all over the world. Were your parents in the service, Coop?"

Coop felt cold, so cold that as he inhaled, his whole self stung. He said, "I lost both my parents. My father was in and out of jail since the day I was born and died ten years ago in a sieve fight and my mother was killed by a hit and run driver when she ran a red light. My grandmother raised my sister and me. I joined the service for something to do. There were no real jobs where I grew up."

"Forget about today, Coop, forget it, throw it out like a piece of junk mail," Morin said in his gravelly voice.

Coop blew smoke into the darkening sky. "I'll guess I'm better."

What was worse was being slashed at by some irrational mother, watching Johns lose it, or having to listen to the morbid smoothness to the staff sergeant's voice trying to make everything appear business as usual. Coop much preferred Morin's style of counsel. At least, he had some warmth. And he looked at the whole thing like no one was at fault; they were all in this together. He didn't push madness to the fringe, the way they used to blame consumption on those with weak chests.

"Everything was in transition," Tanenhaus said.

"To what?" Coop asked.

"Yeah, and why?" Morin asked. "With the kind of pressure we're put under, any one of us could snap. Johns was a good guy, a squared away soldier. Don't let anyone tell you differently, Coop."

"Yeah," Coop said.

"We have to worry about a lot of different enemies," Tanenhaus said.

"I'm not afraid of the Muslims, the Zionists, or the white supremacist," Morin said.

"Morin," Coop asked. "Aren't you white?"

Morin kept talking without missing a beat. "I'm not afraid of the donkeys or the elephant. I'm not afraid of the end or the beginning."

What if what I saw today was the beginning, Coop wondered. Any rational person will tell you it's never a good idea to go into a full-blown panic. A good soldier thrives on disciplined and measured reactions to whatever was thrown his way. But to ignore the graveness of the situation with this lite talk, which was just east of geniality, what could be gained by this? A mother was dead. This was real, not Roswell.

Morin finally smashed out his smoke. "The banks are still sending out solicitations for credit cards. Poor ass me even gets three in one day. When that stops, you know it's over."

Five

Coop rang his sister Marilyn, or as she's known at the gentleman's club, Merry Land. Jarring music blared in the background. AC/DC. "You Shook Me All Night Long."
Coop asked if he'd caught her at a bad time.
"I was just settling in," Marilyn said.
"Regular crowd?" Coop asked.
"A little thin, but hey, it's still early." She was fond of saying, 'hey'. It was to compensate for a stuttering problem she'd had as a child. Since eleven on, it was "hey, this" followed by "hey that" but sadly by that point the damage was already done. The label had been pressed into her by her language arts teachers, branding her not college material.
Minus the learning disability, school wasn't where it was at for Coop either. Coop was so bored attending the too big classes taught by teachers who were disconnected, forever putting in for a transfer to the suburban school district where the student body was larger, more motivated, and less mouthy. But Coop toughed it out and got his diploma, didn't have kids out of wedlock, and joined the service to learn a trade.
His sister, Marilyn, did none of this and things went south. Real south, real quick.
They say that one in four women have experienced sexual trauma in America. Now what that means could be

a range. Anything from upskirting to being the victim of a train. Coop wondered what happened to his sister and he guilted himself over what he could have done. But he didn't know for a fact if anything happened. Coop meant to ask but never did, he always meant to talk to her deeply but rarely plumbed the depths.

"Hey, have you volunteered for any dangerous mission?" Coop hesitated then said. "No, not yet. How have you been?"

His older sister certainly wasn't a sole child who wrestled with speech issues or was raised by her grandmother. So how did things veer off the way they did? This free spirit got through life on her moose good looks. She was never much for formal schooling, but Coop never thought she'd come to this.

Sure, they attended one of those dropout factories. Maybe there were unaddressed emotional issues.

In this land of plenty was the rule of scarcity, old (even then) grandma always did calculations at stores. There was always a fear, a fear of scarcity. I can buy this or that but never both, she would say.

Their grandmother, with her bad knees—even back then, now had a bad heart.

"Hey, one of us had to walk the straight and narrow, Coop, I would have rather it had been me but what's that thing Grandma used to say, wish in one hand pee in the other see which one gets filled first," she said.

He liked it when she got like this, philosophical. Marilyn/MerryLand didn't account for her life like most people. For her, it wasn't about being successful or failing. Or being happy or tragic. It was something else. Something in between.

Her voice went in and out, but it wasn't the connection it was the way she spoke up and down, quietly saying some words then stepping on others.

Coop wondered if she was on drugs then. He always suspected that of her and most of the time he was right.

"It's not too late for you to get out. You could leave any time."

"Yeah. Sure. Hey. What else is there?" she asked. "Hey, I read the Sunday paper. There's a recession going on. Even computer programmers are unemployed."

"Since when were you interested in computers?"

"Hey, who said I was. They promised that was a certain thing. Just like medical transcribe, transcribe-"

"Transcriptionist?"

"Yeah, them."

"What about them?"

"They still have jobs, but for how long? Hey, how long before they're in the unemployment line."

"Marilyn-"

"Hey, it's getting to be that the only people that will be employed will be soldiers and strippers."

"Really?"

"Yeah, really. But, hey, look on the bright side, at least we're not whores," she said with a hardy laugh followed swiftly by a smoker's cough.

Through her phlegm she managed to get out, "Hey, G.I. Jane takes the stage around eleven." Then she chuckled some more.

Coop shook his head as he stood by the window in the barracks. He popped the top of a beer can and slurped the foam off the lid as he watched a bunch of birds change from one pole to another.

"How's my favorite nephew?" Coop asked.

"He's fine. I had him for a few hours last weekend. I rented that movie with the talking dragon. And I fixed turkey sandwiches," Marilyn said. "Open face."

Coop closed his eyes and pictured the faces on the plates, warm, with a little brown gravy on it.

"Your nephew asks for you. He doesn't understand why you've been deployed to Philadelphia."

"That makes two of us," he considered saying but instead a short, heavy silence descended between them. He was puzzled about what was more scarring to his nephew, the fact that his Uncle Coop was assigned to a far-flung place or his private dancer mother only has partial custody of him thanks to her addiction issues. When Coop finally spoke, he opted for a tidy answer in an even voice. "Tell him I'm fine. How did Grandma's doctor's visit go?"

"He always says the same thing about her heart. He did prescribe new meds though."

"Weaker or stronger?"

"Stronger," Marilyn said.

"What are they giving her? Do you remember?"

"I don't. Hey, I have a photographic memory… I just don't have any film," she said whimsically.

"I hope she'll be all right."

"Look, everything will be all right. Or not. I mean, hey, what can we do about it? What? What?" she asked.

More silence.

Coop suppressed a sigh. It would forever irk him. Why hadn't the lone star state worked out for his sister. With her naturally curvaceous figure and caramel skin tone, he figured she could trade on her looks forever. Find a nice, old-fashioned, well-off guy to take care of her—live the American Dream.

But things never quite work out that way. More often than not, the light goes stale and fades. So, Marilyn became Merry Land over the course of time. The first year after her son's birth was harder than she thought to care for a child. It took up so much time and her baby didn't sleep as much as she thought he would. And the guy that she thought knocked her up was cleared by a paternity test. So, she moved to the second suspect and bingo. A match. But unfortunately, the guy's mother fought for custody calling both parents unfit.

So, Marilyn had to fend for herself.

Coop's heart became lighter whenever she spoke of taking classes at the community college–to be a nurse. But that never panned out.

The gentleman's club always hired her back. (And what was the shame of it, nothing. We all have to compromise and lose ourselves a little for employment.) (Aren't we all slipping down a pole, whether we're wearing a thong or not?)

"Marilyn, I better go."

"Coop, you sound weary."

"No, I'm just tired," he said, not realizing he was agreeing with her.

"Really?"

"Yeah, really. Give your son a hug for me next time you get him for part of the weekend."

"Will do… It's not too late."

"Too late for what?" he asked.

She let out this invitation. "You can come over to my side any time you want."

"I don't look so hot in fishnets."

"Funny," she said without a laugh. "You haven't lived until you have rows and rows of cretins looking to you for a deep meaningful overnight relationship."

Over the phone, Coop heard a pounding on a door. "All right, all right, don't blow a testicular," she said to whoever was knocking.

"Marilyn, I better go," he said.

"Wait…So what did you do today?" she said.

Coop whistled in the dark and lied. "Oh, you know the usual."

"You sound like something's wrong. Maybe you need to decompress. Why don't you ask for a few days off?"

"They're not giving days off right now, Marilyn."

"Why not, Coop?"

"They don't have to give a reason; this is the Army."

"Hey, it's not an Army of one."

"Marilyn, what do you think I'm going door to door doing?" Coop asked her.

She didn't have an answer mainly because Coop was always this way with her-sketchy. But what would be the point of unloading on his sister who was an on again off again single mother and worked at Delilah gentlemen's club four nights a week while she pondered finishing her Associates degree in nursing. How could she help? How?

"Coop?"

"Yes," he said.

"Hey. Be careful."

Seven

What was the point? Coop thought as the clock radio beside his bed began to buzz. He quickly shifted the switch to a radio station and a song came in about starting a revolution. It was the oldies station. Followed by another fossil, Patsy Cline's "Crazy." (Crazy for crying/ Crazy for trying…)

Down the hall there was plenty of activity, it sounded like about twenty men were jogging in place then clapping between push-ups. A cadre went by the window chanting "Jodie this and Jodie that. Jodie's got your Cadillac."

Coop sat up in bed then held his face in his hands. His talk with Marilyn had failed to wipe the slate clean. He didn't understand why they didn't give him a few days off to debrief. Even if they did, would even yearsoff decloud him.

Thoughts bubbled. Johns popped into Coop's head. Johns was telling one of those shaggy dog stories in that happy-go-lucky complete with a twinkle in his innocent green eyes delivery he had. Or were they blue? All Coop could de facto recall was how he spoke. So hyped up. So gung ho.

"But don't you see," Johns said, "the zombies were a stand in for Al Qaeda."

Coop listened to this memory till he only heard himself

breathing.

Get a hold of yourself, Coop thought to himself. He had to get that motor mouth murderer out of his head.

Coop felt for his glasses on the nightstand and crawled out of the cold sheets.

He headed into the shower and prepared for the day.

Eight

Now, he worked solo. He drove through streets under the hooded streetlamps. These houses were tightly bound together. The number he sought: 1244 Newell Street. He found it in the end. It had a swing set crammed in its very small front yard.

His heartbeat thickly as he walked up to the door and rang the bell.

A woman with brown hair and wearing a blue terry cloth robe opened the door. "I've been expecting you," she said.

"Is your son available, ma'am?"

She nodded. "Yes, yes. I'll get him."

She leads Coop to a seat on her floral sofa and calls to her son. "Scott," she said in a voice that had a kind of weight to it. A kind of grace.

She looked back over to Coop. "Can I get you anything?"

"No, Mrs. Penderson."

"Dwight." She corrected him and explained, "I went back to my family's name after the divorce. My children kept my ex-husband's name."

Coop nodded. He sat and waited, keeping his eyes trained at the staircase. So far, so good.

Coop noticed things about people, their hair color, their hands, their eyes, the condition of their teeth. In the minutes that he spent in their houses he noted their habits, their knick knacks and curios.

A small head peeked out from near the top.

Coop waved and the whole body emerged. It was a little girl. She gathered the courage to come down and stood before him and giggled.

"Kasidy, your breakfast is on the table," Ms. Dwight said. She took her daughter's hand and led her into the kitchen.

"Hi," a male voice said.

Coop turned and observed the young man full in the face. He was short, about 5'4" but stockily built. He had an unusual face with cheekbones that sort of leap out. His fairish hair had tight curls like a lamb's coat.

"Hi," Coop said.

The mother returned to the room. Her eyelids didn't flutter; she wore just a watchful smile.

Coop turned to give her and her son a private moment. After that time, Coop and the draftee made their way to the car and Coop drove him to the base to get processed. The E-6s, 7s and 8s all nodded accordingly.

Coop didn't dilly dally nor bask in the fact that yes, sometimes they do come quietly.

Then, he pulled out his list to see who was next.

Nine

Coop hammered at her front door. Lucy heard the knock and entered the living room. She wore a fitted red dress under a loose white apron. She opened the door.

"I think you know why I'm here," Coop said. "I'm here on behalf of the United States government with a notice for your son. Is he home?"

She slammed the door.

He knocked again.

"Mrs. Jackson, Mrs. Jackson," he called. "You're just prolonging the inevitable."

She went to the central closet and took out the vac. She began using it on the thinned oriental rug, bumping into the hodgepodge of rummage-store brown furniture.

"Mrs. Jackson. Mrs. Jackson," he called over the noise. She turned on the radio. He banged harder on the door She ignored it.

He went to the window. He lifted it and climbed through. "You really ought to lock that. Anyone can climb through," he told her.

"Any criminal."

"Mrs. Jackson, I'm not a criminal. I represent the United States government."

She spat at him.

He wiped it off with a handkerchief from his pocket.

33

His voice remained low and impersonal. Wide shouldered, he was a good-sized man with a proud carriage. He kept his small brown eyes behind army-issue glasses.

"Kentu Jackson is your son, right? He needs to report To-"

"I've never heard of him."

"Kentu Jackson is your son," he stated.

"I said I've never heard of him."

"Ma'am, this is no time to play games. Every able-bodied man between the ages of-"

"He's not going."

He handed her the paperwork. "Here. Here's the address of the armory. If you need transportation, call this number and transportation will be provided for him."

"I said, he's not going," she said and ripped the paper in half.

He opened up his bag and pulled out a roll of tape. He taped the paperwork back together. He told her, "Well then, he'll be put in jail. Have your son show up on the 22nd. That's the way things are." Coop stiffened. "I'm sorry."

"Are you?" she demanded.

He noticed that her eyes were done up. Kohl blackened that he had only been worn in movies by actresses hoping to get an Oscar. This effect played just as dramatically against her brown skin. "I said I was," he said.

"You know, my father died. He was a marine."

"I'm sure he died a hero."

"He's dead all the same," she told him. "How many homes do you visit a day?"

"You're my eleventh," he told her.

"It ain't even noon."

"I'm highly motivated."

She winked at him. "That I can see. Tell me, what kind of reception are you getting?"

"A little of everything. Some people are like you."

Her eyebrows flew up.

"No matter," Coop continued, "I'm trained to deal with all kinds."

"The old country doesn't work anymore. I hope you know that the public doesn't want this."

"That may be true, but everyone has to do their part. This sacrifice must be shared equally. It isn't like there's some mythical French Foreign Legion that's going to handle all of our business. It's up to us. All of us. Do you have any cash?"

Her dark eyes roved over to him.

"Get some cash together. Have about a month's worth on hand. Get your documents together. Get a sleeping bag. Make sure you have enough kerosene for a lamp."

"Did you round up the two boys on Cherry Street?"

He looked at the list.

"What's the last name?"

She thought for a moment. "Williams. I think."

He nodded in affirmation. "Yep. Vincent and Joseph Williams, 2441 Cherry Street."

"How about that other boy?" She snapped her fingers as she tried to think of his name.

"Can you be more specific?"

"He's about my son's age. He has a funny-shaped head." She demonstrated the way he walked with his shoulders up close to his ears.

"You'll have to give me a name or an address."

"Cherry Street, too. A little bit up the block."

Coop checked his sheet, his nostrils fluttering slightly with his indrawn breaths. "I have a Lawrence Tucker. He's on 2713 Cherry."

"That might be him. How about-"

"Don't you communicate with your neighbors?"

"I don't get out much."

Coop looked around at the bare, textured walls but kept getting back to her. Clothes were on the radiators. Dust balls were the size of borders. This cretin was housed in the corners. Books were strewn everywhere. That body, so strong, so healthy looking, soft, large breasts above a tapered waist above wide, feminine hips.

"My advice to you is to start communicating even if you don't like it. We have to stay connected and create a network."

"What are you talking about?" she asked.

"Survival."

She gazed at him with a lively expression. "Would you like a cup of coffee?"

He scratched his head. "Coffee?"

"Yes. Do you like coffee?"

"You're offering me coffee? Mrs. Jackson, I'm talking to you about emergency preparations."

"How do you like it? Black or with cream and sugar?"

"I like cream. I have to go."

"What's your rush?"

"I have a schedule, Mrs. Jackson. Make sure your son gets that letter. It'll keep him out of a lot of trouble."

She smiled. "One coffee with cream coming up."

Coop's military bearing was all but blown. "Mrs.

Jackson."

"I'll put it in a Styrofoam cup. You can have it to go."

Coop made a notation in his logbook. Lucy tried to snatch the book from him. He pushed her away.

"Can't you wait five seconds? It's just a damn cup of coffee," she shrieked at him.

But before Coop could say anything she back pedaled, lapsing into deep apologies. "I'm sorry. I'm sorry. I'm sorry. Just please. Please. It's only coffee."

Coop imagined her kitchen. More chaos. Coffee boiled, sputtering to the top of the pot, staining the already stained walls. Much like this living room, the kitchen was probably a very dark room. Grime choked out the light. "Mrs. Jackson, I don't want you to go to the trouble of making a whole pot."

"All this is missing is a woman's touch."

"What are you?"

"*I'm* a lady." She smiled and leaned into him. "What do I look like?"

He shook his head and smiled sadly. "You really ought to get some fresh air, Mrs. Jackson."

She gazed at him heartily. "A recruiter. A survivalist and a shirk all in one. This is my lucky day… How old are you?"

"Late 20s. Knocking at the door of 30."

She told him she was pounding on the door of 40. I wouldn't be against war if they took people my age and up. The roster when my father had died, the median age was 22."

"The young fight better. A geriatric soldier ain't much use to anybody."

She nodded. "They take the youngest and the strongest."

He frowned. "Long as they don't take the brightest-"

"My father was 19 years old."

"He must have started early."

"Which one, having a kid or dying?"

"It's a good thing he did reproduce early. If he didn't, I wouldn't be here. If I weren't here, I wouldn't have given birth to my son. And you would have him on your list. Isn't life funny that way? The 22nd, is it? You're going to take my son away."

He tilted his chin up. His jaw stiffened. "I'm not taking your son away."

"The hell you aren't, soldier." Mrs. Jackson said. "I blame the messenger for the message. There is no need for this. We can talk this out."

Coop waved his arms in defeat. "We are tired of that."

"We could try some more," she said. "Offer another resolution."

"You know what you remind me of, Mrs. Jackson, that scientist from *The Thing*."

Her face crinkled into a game lopsided smile. She told him there was no scientist in *The Thing*.

"Yes, there was."

"No, there wasn't. I saw that movie the week it came out. That was when I used to go out."

"How could you? It was made in the '50s."

"It was made in the '80s," she insisted.

"No, it was a black and white film."

"Soldier, it was in color."

"We're talking about two separate movies. In the film that I saw the soldiers have the thing surrounded, and they are about the fire at it. Then this scientist comes running up to the soldiers to stop them. The scientist said, 'Wait a minute. Wait a minute. Maybe we could talk to it.' So the scientist goes running up to The Thing and The Thing knocked him in the head." Lucy explained.

"That doesn't happen in the remake. There's no scientist." Coop said.

"Don't tell me, The Thing doesn't get killed?" she asked.

"Yeah, they killed it, but it still ends kind of dark. They're stuck in this remote Arctic wilderness in front of a dying fire. After they kill the thing, they all think they are safe but then they remember they have no way of getting back to civilization." He asked her what the thing looked like.

This time her cheeks rose with her smile. It radiated lines to the corner of her eyes. "Great special effects. Each time the Thing gets shot it morphed into a dozen other things. Sort of like our foreign policy. The future can be changed. It doesn't have to be war."

"Mrs. Jackson, war brings peace."

"War brings peace?" she repeated making his statement a question. "And people call me crazy?"

Coop gave her half a smile.

She continued to be stuck on that same movie. "After killing The Thing, we're all going to find ourselves huddled around a dying flame. My son is not going to fight in your war. He's a conscientious objector."

"He didn't register as one."

"I didn't know he needed to. He's at a peace rally right now. He's a pacifist."

39

He gave her a pseudo smile. "So am I."

She smiled. "You don't dress like one."

He smiled more fully. "What do you have against the military?"

"It's not so much the military. It's the government."

"This is the United States, Mrs. Jackson, we are the flame of democracy. I'll do this much for you. I'll report that you were nowhere to be found. That'll put him on the bottom of the list. It'll be a month, maybe even two before the next go round. By the time there's a next go around, maybe it'll be over one way or another."

She reached to embrace him.

He stepped back.

"I'm just trying to thank you."

"You don't have to. Just tell your son to be careful at these peace rallies. A lot of people get hurt by them."

"You make it sound like war."

"It's worse than war. They are prolonging things. Your son honestly thinks if he spoke to enough people, he "Could stop the war?"

"My son is a peace fighter. Couldn't you take him off the list altogether?"

"That's all I'm going to do for you. I've got fifteen more houses to get to. I want to get to them before the curfew."

"I'm going to jump out of the window."

He pointed to the window he came in through.

"Make sure, it's that one. There's not much of a drop."

"I'm talking about killing myself if you take my son away from me."

"Ma'am, I did what I could."

"But I'm suicidal, I tell you. Don't you have a pamphlet

in your satchel? Some referral list."

"There's nothing else in my briefcase for you."

"You've got very nice brown eyes. They're very kind. Understanding."

"Mrs. Jackson, I have to leave now."

"Don't they usually send you fellas around in groups of two?" She asked running her fingers through her loose afro-ish hair. Her black hair shone like a newborn animal.

"The short story is we're very short handed."

"Do you think they'll send my son to the front?"

"Mrs. Jackson, there is no front. In case you haven't noticed, we're surrounded from all sides."

"You're gonna put my son in the middle of all that."

"Mrs. Jackson, we're all in the middle."

"He's my son. My only son."

"I understand, Mrs. Jackson. I really do. This is just the way things are. He's got to go. Sooner or later we all will. The William brothers. Tucker with the funny head. Lottie, Dottie, every damn body."

Lucy's kohl eyes appeared sad. "My son is anemic."

Coop gave her a reassuring smile. "We'll feed him steak. Medium rare."

"He's vegan. He doesn't have the temperament. He's my only son. Isn't there a clause against that?"

He stiffened his lips. "Not anymore." He turned and walked to the door.

"Wait. I want to tell you something. I'm not a Mrs."

"I was just being polite."

"Polite? What are you, from the Midwest?"

"Texas."

She brightened. "Oh, a Cowboy. Well, I'm surprised

you don't sound as cornpone as our leader. Can you say nuclear?"

"I never had much of an accent."

"Just say it."

"What?"

"Nuclear."

"Ma'am, please. I don't have time-"

"It's kind of funny. He said nu-clear. Nu-clear. Well, I think it's funny. Here we are on the brink of nu-clear war." She laughed and those crows' feet sprang up on her face.

"If he'd like us to believe it, it would be nice if he could pronounce it." Kentu said. "How many times are we going to go through this? Being lied to, manipulated by our government with these scare tactics."

Coop turned to her. "What makes you so sure this is a scare tactic?"

"What makes you so sure it isn't?"

"I'm an MP, ma'am. I follow orders."

"You're being lied to by this war machine-"

"I have a job, Mrs. Jackson."

"No war for oil."

"That's not what this is about."

"What is this about? Does anyone know?"

He said nothing.

"I thought you had an answer for everything."

"I don't have an answer for that."

"You are a nice-looking young man. Are you spoken for?"

"Mrs. Jackson."

"I'm done telling you, Cowboy-I'm not married-yet."

"Ma'am."

"Call me, Lucy. It's short for Lucia."

"Lucia," he repeated.

"I like when people call me Lucy," she told him, as she went to the door.

"I'm going to stand in front of this so you can't leave. I'm going to be a human shield."

"There's always the window. That's how I came in," he told her.

"I'll be a human shield there too."

"Ms. Jackson…"

She touched the side of his face, "Thank you. Thank you. I knew you weren't a monster."

She grinned.

"I'm a priestess. I'm going to put a spell on you."

As Coop tried to make sense of her words, Lucy was all over Coop. It was too late for reason. She was kissing him. Pawing him. Her dress screamed the color red. She took off her apron and Coop's glasses. Then began to take off her dress.

Ten

Down the hall, a door opened and closed. Telepathy? Was she coming this way? The nurse. Or they? The nurses. Or maybe him? That doctor, with his cozy, fatherly voice. Whoever it was, Coop heard the footsteps.

Closer. He got that sinking feeling then a burning sensation that came up his windpipe and rested in the back of his throat. What the Hell was he thinking?

Hers was the 11th house in less than four hours. So motivated. Johns yapping to slow him down. If he would had just taken a break, perhaps his mind would have been clearer. Maybe he wouldn't have been so susceptible.

But sex. Who wouldn't take up an offer like that? Was there a man on earth that strong? Samson? Napoleon? Bill Clinton? If a woman's going to serve it up for you right there on a platter, who was he to say no?

He had rang the doorbell with all his military bearing. Certainly, he wasn't looking for anything. He was just trying to serve papers.

It was the furthest thing from his mind. No, that wasn't true. He was human, with all that humans want and feel, but he wouldn't have done it if she wasn't so willing.

She flipped everything. He longed to be dominated. It's always the beautiful beginning of the terrible.

Eleven

Back in the ward, the walls of her bedroom were the color of madness. Her ceiling the color of depression. Yellow and blue, respectively. But that was all right because Coop didn't do much sightseeing after the first few moments inside, he realized that maybe it wasn't such a wise move.

Just what was he getting himself into?

Hadn't another mother taken a hatchet to him just a few days before? Didn't his partner wig out and hack that mother to bits?

When was enough already? Weren't there evildoers? Terrorists and the like. Shouldn't he have kept focused on that.

Philadelphia verged in martial law. This was no time to be seduced by the carnal. But that body. That body, so full and welcoming. How her white slip contrasted her rich brown skin. How she twirled her legs in the air.

And her breasts—heavy and shapely, all meat, small nipples—they could make you cry out loud. After the act, he put his face between them and felt the warmth. He remembered thinking this would be the way he'd like to die, not by Al Qaeda but suffocated by all this dense flesh.

From what he gathered, he figured she did this a lot. She didn't give a care to the nation's problems and moreover sliding out of her panties was her way of making sense of the world. And why not? It made about as much sense as anything. He lay on her breasts trying to ignore the pangs of regret he was feeling already.

Recreational copulation wasn't his thing. He was always one of those corny guys who thought he needed to really know the girl beforehand. Is it any better when you care? That night, he finally realized it actually wasn't. Back where he was from there was this saying, "Find them, fuck them and..." it's so hard to abide by that last part. Deep down maybe he was the sensitive type. He hated to take advantage.

Coop relaxed for a moment or two and considered what harm he had done by this. It wasn't like he took advantage of her.

Lucy. What was there was some balloon floating next to her head that read "crazy" and who was he to judge anyhow. Why not bed a stranger after the week he had. What could it hurt? Still, he kept his peripheral vision sharp all the same, suppose she picked this point and time to take leave of her senses: supposed she got up and decided to kill him. What would happen? He'd have to defend himself right.

He didn't get a violent vibe from her. And then she wanted him to talk. And play games.

"Close your eyes," she told him.

"What?"

Her face moved closer to his. "Close your eyes."

"What?"

"Close your eyes."

He shook his head.

She didn't seem disappointed. "Is this your first job?"

"The service?"

She nodded.

He shook his head. "My first job was as a delivery boy. I hated it."

"You mean those desperate housewives didn't leave you a nice tip?"

"The gratuities were good. But their dogs. They were brutal. It seemed like every other house I went to they'd come tearing at me."

"They're just guarding what's theirs," Lucy said.

As night burned into day, they stared at each other again in the missionary position.

And while he had a hold of her warm shoulders, she threw her head back and the dark jungle of her hair fell back clearing her face. She kissed him on the ear and said, "Trust me."

He didn't but remained mute about it and kept on fucking.

It was safer to screw than talk. He closed his eyes.

Twelve

The next morning, her son, Kentu, was on the telephone. He was a short man with a hollowed chest and knobby knees in baggy canvas trousers. He paced as he spoke. He had his mother's big, dark eyes, sans smudged mascara. On the front of his tee-shirt was the word: *Peace.* On the back, it read: *Bush Is WRONG.*

He talked into the phone. "Yes, the buses will leave at seven in the morning. Yes, it's $20 per seat but no one will be turned away due to lack of funds. We need as many people there as possible to declare to the world that this war is not in our name."

His mother, Lucy, entered. She is in just a beige slip which plays warm against her deep skin tone. "Kentu," she said.

"Hush, Ma…" He went back to the phone. The voice on the line told him that five a.m. was too early. "Our government is about to unleash its full might against another third world country don't tell me five is too early in the morning. What? Huh? Take a goddamn nap on the bus then."

"Kentu," she called.

He waved her off. "Not now, Ma."

In his intensity, his shoulders bent forward. "We can't think of our own physical needs right now. Think of the

Iraqis. They have suffered over a decade of war and sanctions. Think of their sacrifices. Think of the Afghans, they don't even have alarm clocks. They don't have beds. They live in abject poverty and squalor. What?" he asked on the phone. "What? I don't care if Seattle is closer, we want to be in the big one this weekend. What? Yes, the San Francisco one is bigger. Yes. All right, all right, we'll leave at 8 then. Is that all right? You spoiled American pig get you're fucking beauty sleep... And don't forget BYOS... Bring Your Own Signs."

He slammed down the phone.

"What do you want, Ma?"

"I just wanted to say good morning."

"There's nothing good about this morning, it's the same old America with the three KKK. (Kentu reads as offensive) The same old economical plunder enforced by military genocide from the Congo to Kashmir. From fucking Chechnya to the fucking Sudan-" He up and downed her. "Where's the rest of your clothes? Don't tell me you got some last night."

She giggled. "All right, I won't tell you."

"Who is it?"

"You'll see."

"He's still here. We'll then it's not the newspaper man. He'd have to be on his round by now. Is it that carpet guy?"

"You'll see."

"It's the carpet man."

Coop walked in the room; he bristled at the sight of Kentu's tee shirt.

Kentu's jaw also dropped. He even staggered back a bit.

Both men peered at each other in a moment of silence.

Kentu spoke first. "A white pig with black skin."

"What?" Coop asked.

Kentu turned to his mother. "Ma, you have really-scraped the bottom of the barrel this time. You bring this slime into this house."

"Slime?" he asked as the words turned in his head. Synapse fired. Coop looked at Lucy.

She said nothing.

Kentu pointed to Coop. "You're lower than slime. You're a puppet. Just like that manufactured enemy by the mobilization of xenophobic, political reactionary flag waving, patriotism. The pressed uniforms. The shiny shoes. The fruit salad on the chest. Trinket medals. This is an outrage. You are such a fucking joke," he turned back to his mother. "Goddamn it, Ma. You are damn desperate." Again, he pointed at Coop. "You're not the first and you will not be the last. Over the course of 19 years I've seen the newspaperman, the carpet guy, and three mailmen. All those poor brothers fell for that crazy lonely bit. Ma, you better bring back that plumber to lay his pipes, because this is totally unacceptable."

Instead of addressing her son she turned to Coop. "How do you like your eggs?"

Kentu paced, eyes flashing.

"Is he for real?" Coop asked her.

"Don't pay any attention to him, Coop, my son is always like this," Lucy said and exited the room, leaving the two of them together.

Kentu gave Coop a hard look, then exhaled loudly. Finally, he said, "She can sleep with whoever she wants. I've got bigger things to worry about."

"You're impeding ship date?" Coop asked.

"I'm not going anywhere. If all goes right, neither will you."

Coop ignored the bitterness in Kentu's voice and kept his own civility. "Diplomatic roads have been exhausted."

"Have they? Have they? Have they?" Kentu asked.

Coop nodded.

"There's still time to talk. I'm joining the blockade. Thousands of us are going to form a human shield."

"You can join hands with your mother."

Kentu shot him a quizzical look.

"You're wasting your time."

"No one said peace is easy."

"Some people make things harder than it has to be. I'll just say goodbye to your mother and leave."

"You don't have to. She is famous for these etch-a-sketch relationships."

Coop shot him a quizzical look.

Kentu snapped his fingers. "You will be forgotten like that."

Coop nodded but went toward the kitchen.

Kentu blocked him. "Don't flatter yourself, Soldier. I told you my mother had plenty of visitors. You can leave without saying goodbye."

Coop halted and looked at Kentu. "I was flattering your mother."

"You know what they say about bread."

"No, why don't you tell me about bread, Kentu?"

"A slice of a cut loaf is never missed."

If it's one thing Coop hated, it was poetry. "And that means?" Coop asked.

Lucy came back in with a tray of steaming hot coffee and toasted toast. "Breakfast is served. Coop, why don't you sit here next to me," she instructed.

"He'd rather have a mess kit and crawl into a foxhole."

She clapped her hands. "Kentu, you sit here."

Kentu stared at the plate contemptuously.

"Who can think of food at a time like this? I've got to get things together for the noon rally."

"Be careful. I know what kind of madhouse peace rallies are."

Kentu scowled. "Like you would ever know."

"I've been stuck trying to police them. You people act like you've lost your minds."

Kentu banged his fist on the table. "We're peaceful, goddamn it!"

Lucy stuck her head out from the kitchen. "Kentu!" she warned.

"He's a warmonger," Kentu told her.

Lucy reentered the room. "Kentu, Coop will think that's all you talk about."

Kentu began to pace. "What else is there to talk about, Ma?"

Coop said, "You're wasting your time. You should spend all of your time preparing."

"You're the one who needs to prepare," Kentu said.

"I am prepared," Coop said.

"Oh, yeah. How much water do you have?" Kentu asked. "How much duct tape do you have? Are your windows sealed up? Tell me at all those checkpoints do you even know what you're checking for? Do you really know what the enemy really looked like?"

Coop up and downed him. "Yes."

Kentu ruefully pointed at him with his grimy, bitten up fingers. "Get your own affairs in order. You got a lot of nerve coming over to people's houses trying to tell us. Who do you think you are?"

"My MOS is-"

"Don't give me that Army talk shit."

"That's the same way my father spoke," Lucy said.

"You never met him, Ma, he died before you were born. The US army killed him."

"What do you mean the army killed him?" Coop asked.

"Exactly what I said. We've given enough to this country," Kentu said.

"I'm getting sick of your 'I gave at the office' way of thinking. I'm sorry about your father, Lucy. This is a whole different thing now. This country needs-"

"Fuck what this country needs. This country brought these things on itself," Kentu said. "The United States has a habit of selling weapons to both sides. My grandfather. In his last letter, he told of how 'Made in the USA' was on every bomb. They sold the bolts and nails that went into the weapons that killed us. We've cornered the market of weapons of mass destruction, Soldier. But you don't believe that. Dare I call it a conspiracy?"

"Conspiracy?" Coop said. "You don't get it. We are in it. We are in it. After everything is settled and calm, we can sit around and sort through each and every point you want to bring up."

"You don't understand-" Kentu began.

"No, you don't understand." Coop waved him away. "Go beat a bongo drum."

"We will derail this globalization movement. Waving an American flag won't make it go away."

"Your methods are just as calculated," Coop told him.

"Well at least I'm not a warmonger," Kentu stepped toward him. "Now, what are you going to do about it?"

"Nothing," Coop told him, still in a flat tone.

"The pressed uniform. The shiny boots. The fruit salad on the chest. Trinket medals. You are such a fucking joke."

"You're the one in the uniform," Coop said. "That tee shirt-"

"What's wrong with this tee shirt?" Kentu asked, stepping back a bit to show it off. He held up his grimy hands as if to say 'ta—da!'

He seemed proud of its logo and its meaning. Coop was overpowered by its smell, like he hadn't washed it for days. Coop knew that smell from when he'd been out on field exercises and had to dig a hole to shit in.

"Well, for one thing it's dated. Haven't you heard there was an election and-"

"I know all about this new tool. He's just window dressing. Some warmed over the sellout from a toothpaste ad. He's not for the oppressed people."

"Oppressed?"

"Look at the history of this country. Terrorism. That is the history. You have the nerve to join this army to rape and pillage."

"Hey," Lucy spoke up.

"Stay out of this, Ma. You don't even know that you've been hypnotized by him."

"I hypnotized her?" Coop asked. "You've got this whole thing backwards."

"You expect me to believe that you are innocent. You with that outfit." Kentu said then eyed his mother. "Why don't you go to a singles bar?"

"I came here to do a job," Coop told him. "I have a summons for you."

"Take that conscription notice, wrap it around your anthrax vaccine, and shove it up your ass."

Coop frowned at the angry, frothing dog of a young man with furrowed brows and filthy clothes which stood before him. Coop tried to maintain his bearing. "I'm going to forgive your words on the count of your youth."

"Forgive me? You ought to hang your head in shame for representing this country. You don't understand!" Kentu screamed.

"Save it for a pamphlet."

"I'm saving it for you."

"I don't want to hear it."

"You are in my house," Kentu told him.

Coop smirked and told him. "I'm in your mother's house."

"So, what does that mean? I can't talk, huh? You're silencing me. You're taking away my first amendment rights. You're not here to talk; you're here to fuck my mother. You mother-"

Lucy said "Kentu-"

"Black soldiers, white wars. The chocolate front. Decades of foreign wars. Your raw naiveté manifested in utter blindness. You're primitive scraping your knuckles across the ground. Once again, once again a predominately white society chooses to send its black male population to fight a war that was distasteful to whites."

Coop listened to Kentu and tried to come up with a comeback. He couldn't think of one, so he listened some more.

"And we don't disappoint, we give them frontline participation," Kentu said, pointing wildly. "And you, you deliver us to them. As if we haven't given enough to this country."

"Kentu, let's change the subject," Lucy said.

Did this happen all the time? Was this life to them? Coop wondered if that was the best she could control him.

"I'm from Houston."

"I bet there are a lot of flags waving there. Bunch of gun toting, flags waving, pickup truck driving Billy Bobs."

"Do I look like a Billy Bob to you?" Coop asked.

"No," Lucy said.

"Control your glandular yearnings." Kentu said. "Do you feel protected in this country, Black man?"

"If what you're saying is true, it's true in military or civilian clothes."

"If?" Kentu asked. "You know it's true."

"Now is not the time-"

"When is the time?"

"After this is over. Obviously," Coop said.

"Obvious to who? After this is over, we will be in the same dungeon we've always been here in Amerikkka with the three kkks."

"I don't see what racism has to do with this."

Kentu said, "You don't want to see what racism has to do with this. You're blind. You and your army uniform, your conscription notices and your lies."

"You're the one who's lying."

"That's your advice to me?"

"You've got your draft greeting. Do what you think you have to do."

"I will not," Kentu said. "I will not capitulate."

"Like I said, do what you have to do. All men of a given age group has entered the drafting. This isn't the Revolutionary War. It's the 21st century. Whites don't pay 300 dollars to be released from service. We are all called up."

"I'm not going."

Coop told him, "Then run. Go to Mexico or Canada."

"That doesn't work so well anymore."

"It works well enough."

Kentu told him. "Draft dodgers need funding."

"If it's all that important to you—you'll find a way. Look at Bill Clinton, he was from a poor family, broken home. He's a good role model for you."

"I guess those two buildings tumbled down on their own."

"White people are at stake. Not us."

"What?" Coop asked.

Lucy spoke up. "He said, 'white people are at stake. Not us.'"

"He heard me, Ma. That was an attack against the government, not us. But thanks to sellouts like you, the misery will be spread to us. Thanks to you, caskets will return filled with the remains of African Americans."

"No blacks died in the World Trade Center? Or the Pentagon? Huh? Where's your answer to that?"

"I just gave it to you."

"You are so confused," Coop told him.

"I assure you my thinking is clear."

"Maybe you're thinking clearly, but your talk is full of shit."

"You're the one that's brainwashed, Soldier. I am an African."

"You are an American to them," Coop said.

"Them is us," Kentu told him.

"Us is us," Coop shouted. "And they are them."

"They got to you. As the sun glistened off your armor, Gunga Din. Go ahead and fight for the empire. Meanwhile, us indigenous minorities can't even get a meal at Denny's. The British, the Germans, and the French. The Fucking Portuguese."

"What century are you talking about?" Coop asked.

"While they lulled us to sleep with all their men bitten by shark stories and senators sleeping with intern crap, all this was being plotted. Our Government-"

"Stop right there."

"Just like Pearl Harbor. It's true," Kentu said.

"NYC. DC. This was the worst day in the history of our county."

"I guess Rosewood doesn't count. How about Black Wall Street? How about the bombs in Birmingham?"

"We face biological, chemical attacks- We didn't face that in Alabama. For Christ's sake, what do you want to do, leave Jihad factories to incubate for another 10 years?" Coop asked.

"You don't actually believe that bullshit about 10,000 luscious virgins for them in heaven. I'll tell you why they kill; they have nothing to live for. They call them sand niggers."

"Who are they?," Coop asked.

"This country is chronically racist, sexist, and homophobic," Kentu said.

"I'm not. I'm just trying to do my job," Coop said. "And stay alive."

"Your job kills people, solider. You make sure people are signed up to go halfway around the world and make things go 'boom'. Your hands are drenched in blood. The blood of other people of color. Other brown people getting robbed of their land," Kentu said wildly, gesturing at Coop.

"America must be stopped. Before this world was like us. Starbucked. Big Mac Fucked. The world is not for sale. You want to avoid terrorism? Do you?"

"Stay away from tall buildings and white people. If you do those two things, you will be alright."

Coop said, "That's it. That is it." He rooted in his briefcase for Kentu's taped together paperwork then ripped again. "You don't want to go, Kentu. Don't go."

Kentu pointed. "Don't think there's not a backup somewhere in HQ."

Coop saw the wrinkles on Kentu's already flaring nose. The air flowed in and out in a pumping fashion. He had so much energy about him. Oddly, Coop thought of Johns right then.

"I don't want that boy over there with me. He might shoot the wrong direction," Coop said, making up his mind.

"Who are you calling, 'boy'?,"Kentu asked.

"Are you leaving?," Lucy asked.

"Who are you calling, 'boy'?,"Kentu asked again.

"You're going over there?," Lucy asked.

"Who are you calling, 'boy'?" Kentu asked.

"Kentu, leave Coop and I alone for a few minutes," Lucy told her son. Coop noted as he exited the room that Kentu with his scrawny body didn't even look like he was part of the same species as his lusty built mother.

There was a long heavy silence between Coop and Lucy. She said, "You didn't tell me you were endangered of being shipped out, Coop."

"What do you mean I didn't tell you? I just met you. There's a lot of things I didn't tell you."

Lucy screamed. "You just met me. You just fucked me. When is your ship date?"

"Lucy, this is not-"

"Don't tell me. Don't you tell me what this is, or this is not. When do you ship?"

"Calm down first," he told her.

"Answer my damn question."

"Not until you calm down."

"What difference does it make if I'm calm or not?"

He went to the door.

"Where are you going? Where do you think you are going?"

"This was just a temporary assignment. I ship on the 26th."

"That's too soon. "

"My mission is to secure-"

"I don't want to hear about your fucking mission."

"No, I guess you don't."

Coop turned to leave.

Thirteen

Coop still had the company's(the government's)car. Though he had no idea how he was going to explain these unaccounted miles to his superiors, he drove aimlessly. He was way out of the perimeters, down City Line Avenue. He guided into the Soft Touch Carwash to have the car done, half hoping that high-pressure hot water could scour him alive. He could go under the springs meant for wheel wells and tire rims. He nixed that idea and tried to get situated, riding the city, the burning cusp past all the Saint Joe University paraphernalia. Banners in red and white. At least, America's colleges were still going strong. Public schools had fallen to crap, for now at least, private universities were the envy of the world.

Maybe even that was hype.

Coop drove some more and then some more and then some more. His face felt hot.

He couldn't do it. He couldn't. No more reports written, not tonight. No. There were no words to describe what he was doing anyway.

Watching the Specialist type away little sentences—weren't they all beyond that.

Coop loosened his green tie.

He turned at Lancaster Avenue. In moments, he was almost back to work. All of a sudden, he found it hard to breathe, so he pulled over. He got out to stretch his legs. There was a little strip mall just ahead. A bookstore of which he'd first only window shopped, but then he went indoors. He went over to the café. They were all out of bottled water, but they did offer him a double latte. Passing on that, he moved through the store finally finding a water fountain and took huge gulps from it.

    The clock read 4:30 p.m.; still time to make the tail end the after actions report. Coop felt his grasp on awareness waver. Coop's mind raced. Could he easily explain his lateness? He could say he stopped for an oil change or a tire rotation or tell the truth, and say he went through a car wash. Or he could just breeze right in. What static would they give him after all he'd been through? He saw a woman hacked down in cold blood. Would they have the chance to break his balls over his whereabouts—well this was the U.S. government he was talking about.

    What to do? He never knew what to do.

    So, he got back into the car and circled back to the center of the city.

    The sun went down and the cold increased. He parked, leaving the car near Broad Street and headed down the stone and steel of the city. The brick and asphalt.

    The closed and the abandonment. Business was sour. It seemed every other store front was boarded up. One long dark street led to the next, but there was hardly any bustle to the business district, just a few indigent looking folks milling about the edges. One pushed a shopping cart from Walmart. That store unfortunately folded too. It seemed that every other storefront was abandoned. Down the jewelers' row, there were empty neckline busts and bare statues hands, all gray, gray—empty of diamonds. On the windows, were brown wallpaper, so no one could look inside. Coop, not being a native of this city, couldn't tell what those stores were.

What is a city without business?

This was all too depressing, so Coop ducked into a neighborhood bar called McGlinchey's. It's bannered to be one of the oldest taverns in Philadelphia.

Coop found a seat at the end of the bar as he eyed an American flag on the wall. His eyebrows lowered and became drawn together to form a 'V' on the lower part of his forehead, just above the nose. It was all too much, all this that was happening in defense of this thing. Beginning to sweat, he got up and hit the streets again.

America. America. America. How Coop wished he could take a vacation from it.

More wondering. More wandering. Up Market Street. Down Chestnut Street.

Till it was close to seven and he was sure the high Es had left the board room. Coop moved further up town. This time he ducked into a fancy hotel lobby where the meet up crowd was desirable and fashionable.

It was warm with slabs of maple burning in the fireplace. He guided into a dark cool lounge where the smell of citrus fragrances and shoe polish tainted the air. A tingling piano played in the center of the room further encircled by smattering of women, forty-something to fifty-something women in green or blue pantsuits.

As one of these women stepped to the side, Coop saw the incredible.

Coop's heart jumped.

The piano player had cool green eyes and his singing voice had a grating New York nasality. But it couldn't be…

"Johns?"

The man blew a big cloud of smoke above his head, and he crushed out his cigarette. The man broke up his voice. "Coop-er."

A few of the pantsuits tuned to Coop, annoyed that he'd broken up the musical flow.

Johns motioned that he needed a break to the maître'd and rose from his bench.

Coop followed Johns to a side room.

"How did you escape?" Coop asked once inside.

John's face wore a mild smile. He took off his suit coat and hung it on a padded hanger.

"People turn their backs sometimes," Johns said.

"That's how you slipped?" Coop asked.

He nodded, lighting a whole new cigarette. He took this to his mouth and drew in and out.

"Shit. Where are my manners?" Johns asked. He dug in his vest and offered Coop a smoke.

Coop took it.

"Well, how did you land here?" Coop asked, between puffs.

Johns paged through some sheet music. "I've been playing piano since I was five years old. My mother used to tell me all the time—I have the fingers of a piano player or a surgeon."

"Then why did you join the army?"

"Because my country needed me," Johns said. "Now, I've moved on to plan B."

"You can't be serious."

"Of course I am. My sister was a prodigy, she's at Julliard now. Have you heard me? I'm no Billy Taylor but I'm pretty damn good."

Coop shook his head. "What about the woman you killed?"

"You don't know what's it's like, Coop, just the other night a guy came in and heard me and said, 'Man what are you doing here?'"

Coop frown. "He didn't know the half of it."

"Coop, I'm just playing my set, afterwards having a hamburger and a beer, and then lights out. I'm not hurting anyone. Like when I was a kid when things got too tough my dad used to pack us up in the station wagon and head down to Coney Island, as if salt air could solve anything. I only wanted to help people. Before the army, I was an EMT. I once saved a-"

"Johns, you killed a woman."

"I didn't mean to. If that means anything. So what's this all about. What, are you tracking me down? You're going to leave me to the tender mercies of JAG, or what?"

"I didn't know you were here. I had no idea, Johns. I just happened here."

"That's quite a coincidence."

"Yeah," Coop took another drag. "What's your plan?"

Johns laughed. "Plan? This is my country."

"Johns, you killed a woman in cold blood."

Johns' voice changed and became almost tender. "I going to have a baby."

"What?"

"My girlfriend is two weeks along."

"That's kind of early to check."

"Oh, she's beautiful. I liked the way she wore her hair pulled back, so it fell on her shoulder. Plus, she had a nice pair of tits. We've had our share of ups and downs but I think we're genuinely moving toward a really golden part of our lives." His eyes were bright, and his gestures were expansive. Warm and gushy.

So cheerful and straightforward.

"Johns, I don't understand."

He took a breather and said, "I have an uncle John-"

"John?"

He nodded.

"He has the same last name as you?"

He nodded again.

"You have an uncle named John Johns?"

Johns lifted his eyebrow. "What's the matter with that?"

"John Johns. Having that passenger die on his bus was the lucky thing."

"For the guy who died?"

"No, it didn't work out so well for him. But for my uncle, He got special permission to go on paid leave. It was like they were afraid that other passengers might die. All the passengers look like ghosts," Johns rattled off.

Coop nodded. He definitely wasn't fumbling for words.

"So, he's crazy like a fox."

"No," he looked down. "He's really crazy."

"I thought you said it was good luck."

"Well," he said. "At least he doesn't have to drive the city bus."

"It's like that song."

Coop pressed his eyes closed. "What song?"

"About blessing America."

"God Bless America," Coop said.

"Not that one,"

"God Bless the USA," Johns said confidently.

"You mean, God bless America."

"From the lakes of Minnesota," Johns said whimsically.

"From the mountains to the prairies," Coop corrected.

"No, No. No. The line goes, 'I'd gladly stand up and defend her'."

"Who?" Coop asked.

"America," Johns said as if it was so obvious. He stretched out his knuckles.

Another tuxedoed man came to the door and held out five fingers.

Johns nodded and drained the rest of the water from his glass, pausing a bit to tell it flowed down his throat.

He rose from his chair.

Coop pulled him back.

"Johns, you killed a woman," Coop said.

Johns looked down for a moment before letting his eyes connect again with Coop. "I didn't mean to."

He got up to move again.

"Wait."

"Let me explain."

He paused and swallowed.

"Just give me a second to frame my thoughts: you have to believe me; I love this country."

Someone knocked on the door.

Johns peered at the door then Coop then back to the door. "It's show time."

"Johns, you have to tell me-"

"Sorry, some other time."

Night settled in and the music poured out. Johns was better this second set. He did a cover of that very old Japanese song "Sukiyaki" only he sang it in English. His voice was loose and lush as he seemed to muse over each syllable of the breezy bittersweet tone of the Kyu Samato.

The pant-suited ladies leaned on their elbows at the piano. Coop lingered by the door. He listened and called to mind: It's just a full-time job. It's just a full time job. It's just a full time job.

Johns batted his eyelashes as he sang and connected with the crowd.

Coop watched like a fly bumped up against the window. Maybe everyone is an onion, Coop thought. Everyone has layers and layers and layers. Take enough petals off and you might find a cold-blooded killer or a semi-gifted singer and piano player. He wanted to leave but something about the nice, understated style of conveying emotion and the way he had homing in on his face then turning away.

Maybe he was mixed up.

Did it happen?

It couldn't. This man before him looked so collected. So serene was an insane knife wielding murderer.

He didn't seem like the type who would flip and dice up some lady. Not with that vibrato.

Fourteen

That night Coop heard Johns' voice in his head.
Over and over and over.
It was always the same stopping at the same catch-phrase– "Don't you get it — *Zoombies are a stand in for–*"
Zoombies are a stand in for…
Zoombies are a stand in for…

Fifteen

Long ago, in his youth, the doctor had a boneless, hang-loose way about him. Since then, thirty four years had passed and his posture had taken on a more hunched, tight, wizened stance. He saw patients back to back but tried not to let that show in his voice, which was good when he stopped by his stricken blind patients for all they had to go on was that sound, Coop. He used to not see people like Coop. A survivor. He was used to the malingerers. Those who wanted to get out of service, they pretended to have a bad back, or pretended they couldn't walk, or even pretended to be blind (they didn't know that there were tests that he could take to see if they could see no matter how many times they claimed they couldn't read the chart.)

But under the occupation he met a new breed.

Coop never asked the usual question—"will I see?"

What would be the point of that?

The doctor knew medicine isn't a science; it's an art. So, why bother asking, when he'd get well or even if he'd get well. He didn't have much conversation for the doctor, he just smelt the dust and floor polish.

To inquire when he could see even a stale faded light instead of all the darkness upon darkness upon darkness. Of course, the bandages hadn't come off, when they did, he wouldn't see black he'd see gray when he opened his eyes.

"Nurse, where are the results of the last tests?"

Sixteen

Coop remembered when he slept with her. Lucy grabbed his arm and demanded, "Wait. Wait. Will you wait one minute? Give me. Give me. Give me. One minute of your time."

After she was sure that he was still, she left the room. She came back carrying his glasses.

"On the nightstand, you left this behind. You must not need them," she said softly.

"Just to see things at a distance."

"I have great vision. I could have gone to flight school. Clear. 20/15."

"You mean 20/20."

"20/15," Lucy corrected.

"20/20 is perfect."

"20/15 is better than perfect."

Coop reached for his glasses. She held it just out of reach.

Lucy tried on his glasses. "You know what they call these. BC glasses."

"Before Christ?" she asked.

He laughed. "No, birth control. Because they're so ugly."

"BCG's, eh?" She wondered aloud. "I hope they worked last night…"

Coop's pulse raced. "You told me you were menopausal."

"I lied."

"Just give me the glasses," he told her.

She took them off but again held them just out of reach.

"I used to be just like you. Nearsighted. Then I took a course."

"A course?" he asked.

"An eyesight course. It was only two sessions. Thirty-eight dollars at the Upper Moreland Learning Tree."

"What do you learn in an eyesight course?"

"I just told you. How to see. If you're bad at it. You have to train yourself."

"You trained your eyes to see for thirty-eight dollars."

"Plus, a five-dollar material fee."

"What kind of material?" he asked.

"An eye chart. I remember the day I had of my breakthrough. I had been practicing my eye lessons all summer long and it all clicked for me.

She covered one eye and mouthed the letters. "X J L A 2 R Z."

She covered the other eye. "X J L A 2 R Z. It was a miracle…Not really. It's not honestly a miracle. All I do is trace around the edges of things. I don't see things. You see, seeing is psychological."

"Lucy, seeing is seeing."

"No, you just think it's here." She pointed to his eyes.

"But it's actually here." She pointed to his head. "You see, Coop, maybe there's some things you don't want to see. Maybe there are some things you like to remain fuzzy."

Coop nodded. "All I have to do is believe, and I can

change the shape of my eyeballs."

"All you have to do is believe, and you can have anything you want. Believe, not wish. Believe. I believed that I would meet someone special. Someone I could connect with and talk to. He came right to my door. I didn't wish I believed, Coop. Believe me those other guys are just guys. You are what I believe in…." She licked her lips. She came toward him. "Do you have to go? Do you really have to go?"

"Lucy, I have orders."

"I know. I know. You have orders from headquarters. When they say jump, you ask how high…. Well, here, take your glasses."

He took them but didn't put them on.

"Can I give you something else?" she asked. She took off the beige, silk scarf from around her neck and handed it to him.

He smiled thinly. "It's very nice."

"I hope it reminds you of me."

"Thank you."

"Just one other thing. Take this."

She took off her gold ring from her right hand. "It's my granny's wedding ring."

"You're giving me your granny's wedding ring?", he asked. "You don't seem like the granny's wedding ring type."

"For luck."

"For luck."

"You're repeating what I said."

"You just don't seem like the granny wedding ring type, Lucy." Coop told her.

"You think I never had a granny?" she asked.

"I didn't say that." He worked the ring around in his hand, then gave it back to her. "I can't take this."

"Take it."

"I can't. You keep it."

"Take it. Take it. Take it. Take it to some foreign land. Afghanistan. Uzbekistan. Isbucastan, but I don't understand why you must take a stand in some foreign land- Get the clap from some whore. Go ahead, take it. Please," she shouted.

The crazy Lucy is back, he thought and headed for the door.

"Coop. Wait. You haven't had breakfast. Can I wrap you a muffin?"

Coop walked faster.

"Coop, wait. Wait. Wait. Don't open that door."

Lucy ran to the drawer.

Coop spun around in time to see her pull out a gun. His eyes connected with the weapon.

She cocked it, then laughed. "You're not going, Coop."

"Where did you get a thing like that?" he asked.

"I've always had it."

"I didn't ask you that."

She continued to smile as she cocked the gun. "In this world of uncertainty, a woman needs some protection."

"You don't see me aiming anything at you. Put the gun down, Lucy."

"Coop, I've got you cornered."

"Drop it!" he told her.

She laughed again. "You know the funny part about this. I don't know where my father drew his last breath.

The village. It's not even on the map. I couldn't find it. Forty years later, Nam is a tourist trap. You can book a cruise to it. That's what will happen to Baghdad. The same thing will happen to Isbucastan. What the hell is an Al Qaeda? Huh? What's a Jihad? I don't know any of this?"

"Where did you get that gun?" Coop asked.

"It's Kentu's."

"Kentu? Your son, Kentu, the peacenik?" He stepped toward her.

"It's Kentu's, and it's loaded. I'll prove it. I'll shoot up into the ceiling."

"Then you'd have a hole in your ceiling. Just put down the gun."

"Don't reach for this," she warned him. A little froth was at the corners of her mouth. She ordered him to put up his hands.

"This isn't a game, Lucy."

"Do I look like I'm playing?"

"Give me that weapon."

"Make me."

Coop squared his shoulders, silently and charged her. He grabbed her gun arm and took the gun from her. They struggled briefly. Lucy was scratching, slapping, cuffing, ripping, and tugging at Coop.

She fired at the ceiling. Glass shattered.

"What the fuck?!" Kentu screamed.

"It is loaded," she said.

Kentu stormed downstairs, bleeding a little where the bullet winged him and charged at him. Coop fought him off with one belt, an uppercut that sent Kentu soaring upward. Coop marveled at what a bantamweight Kentu was.

Coop's voice rose and got wild as theirs. "Stay away from me both of you, you're crazy."

Kentu came back to his feet. "Look who's talking? You shot a hole in the roof."

"What in the Hell are you doing with a weapon?" Coop asked.

"You said it yourself. Those peace rallies are no joke," Kentu said.

"Wrap up your hand to be on the safe side."

"I'll live."

"Do you have any dressing?"

"Somewhere…"

With his free hand, Coop reaches for his bag. He threw it to Lucy. She caught it.

Lucy began to rummage through the bag. Kentu held up his good hand to stop her.

"Keep it. We don't want anything from you."

"Lucy, his wound needs to be cleansed, then dressed to prevent infection."

"We don't need anything from you," Kentu said.

"Get it, Lucy."

"No."

"Do as I say, Ma."

Lucy took out the dressing. Kentu rushed up to her, stuffed the dressing back into the bag threw it at Coop.

"Suit yourself, bleed to death if you want to."

"Go to Hell, GI Joe."

"What would it have killed you to follow my instructions?"

Kentu nodded. "Yes, it would."

Coop gathered his bag to leave. He did this with one

hand for with the other he was still holding the gun.

"Coop, don't leave. I don't know what I'm doing. I'm so crazy with–"

"Let him go, Ma," Kentu said.

Coop said, "I'm getting the Hell out of here."

"Coop, no, I don't know what I'm doing I'm so crazy with-"

"Let him go, Ma."

Lucy pleaded, "I thought I was in the country. I'm suffering from shell shock. You can't leave me, Coop. You belong to me. You belong here. You can't go there and live in a tent. You need a home. You don't have a home. You've got a base. You've got a unit. You've got three hots and a cot. I'd rather shoot you then let you out there and die. Die anonymously. For some, a vague notion of freedom, justice-equality."

"The kind of freedom, justice, and equality we have never known," Kentu said.

Coop aimed the gun at them. And all but fired it. He was that demented in that moment. Bestial. Vicious. He had almost forgotten he was in full uniform. At that moment, it came back. 'It' meaning his sanity. Of course, sanity is a relative term. It means different things to different people at different times.

Coop opened the weapon and took the bullets out. He placed the empty gun on the table, then he left, slamming the door.

Behind him, he heard the words: "You can't leave me." Then "MA!"

Then "You belong to me, Coop. You belong here."

Seventeen

Back in the sick ward, there was a fire crackling in Coop's mind. That's what it felt like when drugged or hypnotized.

A fable of fears. (A nightmare is just a type of dream.)

All he could do was notice the texture of the voices about, imagine their innocence or guilt or neutrality.

The touch of a nurse's hand shocked him.

What did she want? What does anyone want?

He shuddered.

Eighteen

Three weeks later, Coop lay in a VA Hospital bed. His eyes were bandaged. The doctor came into the room.

"Good afternoon, Sergeant Cooper. I'm Doctor Kennedy."

"Doc?" Coop asked.

"I'll cut right to the chase. Due to the injury you have sustained, you have a fifty-fifty chance of regaining your sight."

"Fifty-"

"Fifty… Fifty-fifty." The doctor frowned thoughtfully.

"Only fifty percent?"

"Try to look at the glass as half full."

"I don't even remember the blast."

"Maybe that's for the best."

"Doc, I-" Coop began.

"Don't. Not now. Just try to rest. The bandages will be off in a few days and then you can start piecing things together."

"But, Doc, what happened to the rest of my unit? Are they here?"

"Sergeant Cooper, please don't exert yourself."

"Could you at least tell me what happened to Salles? Manuel Salles. His wife is seven months pregnant-"

"Sergeant Cooper, please."

"Can you answer me?"

"You're overexerting yourself. It is important to stay still."

"But do you know anything about him? Or Morin? Wally Patrowski."

"He's a Specialist, Doc."

"Sergeant Cooper, please."

"What?"

"I've always been called Coop, even before I swore in..."

"You can keep calling me Doc, instead of Dr. Kennedy, Coop."

"I don't remember it. I don't have anything."

"That's probably a good thing."

"God, God, I have to know what happened. I need to know what went on."

"Coop."

"Doc, is there a newspaper around?"

"Coop, we have notified your family about your injury. They want to come to visit you, but they were warned not to. What with us being in Code Orange."

"My grandmother wasn't supposed to be notified. She has a bad heart. I filled out forms."

"We told your sister, she and your nephew wanted to come. They left you a package and some letters. Your family will be here as soon as they can. In the meantime, you have a visitor."

"Someone from the unit?"

"I'll send her in."

"Her?"

"Coop," a weirdly happy voice said.

He felt the stroke of her hand. He heard her chuckling

and kissed him. He put it together. "Lucy?"

"I'll leave you two alone," The doctor said leaving the room.

"I wanted to be there when you woke up," Lucy told him.

Coop sat bolt upright. "Doc, no wait. Wait."

"Coop, he's gone. How do you feel?"

He felt her breath on his face. "Blind," he said.

"That's not a feeling,"

"Are you telling me, Lucy?"

"Everything will be alright, Coop. I'll take you home, we'll be together."

"But I don't-" he began.

"Yes, yes, you do, Coop, you just don't know it yet."

"But what about-"

"Cooper, I saw to everything."

"I will read you the paper in the morning and give you a warm bath at night." She stroked his cheek. He lay still beneath her.

"But you're crazy."

"That may be true. I can take care of you. I'm very functional that way."

"I can't remember what happened."

"What does it matter now? We're together. I've missed you so much."

The hospital bed was railed like a crib. She climbed over the guards, climbing on top of him.

"Watch a minute. Ain't we still in the hospital? Wait a minute. Are we in this room alone? Wait a minute."

Lucy kissed him wildly till his opposition was mute.

89

Nineteen

Whenever he woke up, he felt like he was in jail. The sensation of this, the fear lasted only a few seconds, tormented moments. Then he lapsed back into his blind reality in a slow, jolting drive.

Someone down the hall was coughing and coughing. The rasping suck of air over and over.

Followed by no movement of life and the smell of cinnamon. The walls were treated with it.

The bandages feel tight, and he thought about the milky way with its swirls and dips. He should have become an astronaut. Sure, even NASA had its cutbacks, but they could have fit him in, couldn't they? And wouldn't that be a great place to hide, outer space. To get away from the world and come back later when everything was settled.

He jammed his hand under the pillow and flipped it around to the cool side and wrapped himself in the blanket, he almost felt protected.

He shouldn't have enlisted in the military. People are too unpredictable. Too hard to control. Instead he could have been with inflated gray whirls.

Space.

Safe space.

Silent safe space.

He always did well in science. Not so well in math, but

he loved reading about the why of things. And he was right there in Texas. The Johnson Space Center was right on the parkway. If he stayed in Houston, maybe he wouldn't have a problem.

Twenty

Coop touched the shiny glass of the television screen. A classic Jerry Springer was on where a man who believed he was a dog proceeded to be led around by a leash, to lick his master's shoes, and to drink from the toilet bowl.

When he heard Lucy enter the room, he said, "You said you would read me the paper."

"You don't want to do that there's nothing but that war jazz."

"I'm interested in that war jazz."

"Your TV is stuck on UHF. All I can get is Jerry Springer."

"The knob broke."

"Why don't you have a remote control?"

"The same reason I don't have a cell phone. I'm not a bougie." Lucy said.

"Dammit," Coop said. "How are we supposed to know what is going on in the outside world?"

"Exactly," Lucy nodded.

"That's my question."

"That's my answer. I don't give a damn about the outside world."

"You're talking like a-"

"Crazy person. Coop, turn the record over."

He winced. The sound of her voice was eating into him

like acid.

"Lucy, you have to communicate with the outside world. The whole city is in a state of emergency."

For some reason, she laughed. They say crazy people laugh for no good reason.

"There you are harping on that again. You're going to make me forget why I love you with all your nagging and pestering. Relax, will you."

"You just can't close things out like they don't exist."

"Calm yourself. The doctor said-"

"You know what, you need some more grapes."

"I want today's paper. I have to know what's going on."

"Fine. I'll ask."

"I don't want no grassroots zine; I want a newspaper."

Kentu stalked in. "One newspaper. Anything else?"

Coop looked around wildly.

"What's the matter?" Kentu asked. "You didn't hear me come in."

"Take down a list, Kentu. Bring him whatever he wants," Lucy instructed.

"How are we looking at water?"

"The sink worked fine."

"Bottled water."

"The sink worked fine."

"This is in case-"

"I don't drink bottled water."

"Whose list is this?"

"I told you. I ain't busy."

"You need a private supply of water in case-"

"There is nothing to worry about."

"How in the Hell do you know?"

"I'll get you the water. Ma, why don't you leave Coop and I alone for a few minutes."

Lucy left the room whistling "Someday My Prince Will Come."

"Do you get anything to seal up the windows? Do you have any duct tape?" Coop asked Kentu.

"We don't even have any scotch tape."

"Call the VA. I want to go back."

"Three days, and you're all ready to go AWOL."

"Some people aren't meant to live together."

"You're right about that… Still I didn't think it would go this way. All this disharmony. I thought things would be more civil now that you've been declawed."

"Declawed? I didn't know I was ever clawed."

"A blind soldier doesn't hold much of a threat."

"I was never a threat, Kentu. I was fighting for you."

"I never asked you to."

"Maybe, you don't know what's good for you."

"And the United States military does? Let's stop right there before we get into it again."

"I want peace as much as you-" Coop told him.

"Then stop right there. You don't need to go any further. What else do you want from the store?"

"I'm thinking. My mind is so confused. I just don't understand. What would it hurt to get a survival kit together?"

"You're such a hypocrite. You left us here with a hole in the roof and an empty gun and you want to talk about survival."

"Do you have a flashlight?"

"You sound like a Cub Scout with your canteen full of

water and your flashlight. Ask about bullets. That, I did restock."

"What kind of pacifist are you?"

"I never said I was an anti-war, Soldier. I'm anti-establishment."

"You're anti-America."

"Bingo," Kentu cheered.

"I thought you didn't want to argue."

"I don't. I'm just stating the facts. Now you see the end result of bombing your way into popularity. 30% of US Gulf War veterans are receiving disability benefits from injury. Physically or physiologically maimed in a war for big oil. The PAWR. I just find it ironic. Your disability. Your blindness, be it temporary or not. Blind."

Kentu said this word over Coop's shoulder. Coop turned.

"Blind."

Kentu said this over Coop's other shoulder. Coop turned again wildly to track him.

"We have overthrown the democracies in Chile. How about Iran? If we didn't side with Iraq over Iran, there would be no Saddam. And all those puppet governments in Latin America."

"It was all about oil, right?"

"The Kuwaitis fled the country and hung out in discos till we got it sorted out. They have a disco problem."

"Couldn't two things be true at the same time? We fought for access to oil and liberation. If China or Rwanda slaughtered 100,000 or so of their own people, no one condemned it. If the U.S. government so much as accidentally bombed an aspirin factory-"

"Those countries don't purport to be the world's police."

"These countries cause their own starvation, Kentu. If they, as a matter of fact, cared for their children's well-being, they would cooperate with us. If they did that, they'd have all the bread they need."

"Levee."

"What?"

"They don't eat bread. They eat levees."

"They'd have all the peanut butter and jelly on the levee they want."

"The US was right to drop the atomic bombed on Hiroshima and Nagasaki."

"We wouldn't have if they would have cooperated."

"Blindly, do what they say?"

"They are us, Kentu. Cooperate."

"Rebel."

"You remind me of those Hollywood types who never met an anti-American cause they didn't like."

"What's there to like about America? This is a capitalistic hell. America creates the world's misery. Do you know how many children in this world die of diarrhea? America doesn't give a shit about that, excuse the pun."

"America provides ninety five percent of the aid to the world."

"Amerikkka with the three KKKs is evil and if you can't see that you are blind in more ways than one."

"Talk about the pot calling the kettle black. Kentu, you quote your warmed over left-over freeze-dried hippie philosophy at me. You wouldn't know an original thought if it came up and pissed on your shoes."

"It may sound like yesterday's phrasing, but it's as current as today's news. What did you expect from a marching band? If you were Irish, they would be bagpipes. Or was it Scottish. Maybe it was both."

"I expected to be spit on at the airport by spoiled, cowardly, want to be eggheads like you and a ten percent discount on an oil change when I show my military ID."

"I am not a coward. I'm anti-imperialism, Zionism, FBI, CIA. I don't care if I die. It's what I die for that concerns me. I'm not dying for this country. America is the schoolyard bully that beats everyone up and steals their lunch money."

"We have saved the world not once but twice. Maybe you'd like to be speaking German or Russian."

"I'd like to speak Swahili."

"Then, Kentu, take a night class. And while you're at it buy a plane ticket. Go. Go to your communistic utopia."

"I'm not so sure Communism is such a bad idea. It's better than this wretched, servile, fatalistic regime I'm living under here. You act like you're not part of the problem. You and your uniform."

"My uniform? You've been wearing that same peace shirt since I left," Coop accused.

"How can you tell? You can't see."

"No, but I can smell."

"You think this is some kind of joke. This is serious and it's going to get more serious. All those neurological problems, the shortness of breath, sleep disturbances, skin rashes-"

"What are you talking about?"

"Gulf War Syndrome," Kentu said.

"There's a thousand explanations for that."

"Exposure to environmental particles. Uranium. The blitz of inoculations. Seven shoots in one day. How can your immune system absorb that? I heard about this man who came back from the Gulf and his first child was born with six fingers on his hand."

Coop nodded. "Better six than four."

"How about the attack on Iraq, all it did was make martyrs out of the Iraqis, divert our attention from, further empower Al Qaeda, and weaken our standing with our allies."

"Maybe, Kentu, if we had your help things would be over by now."

"Take that conscription notice, wrap it around your smallpox vaccine and stick it up your ass," Kentu told Coop. "For more than 30 years now, we've started things up in the Middle East to ensure peace. Fifty years ago, we sacrificed more than 50,000 lives to protect the South half of Korea."

"That's our role, to monitor and overt all threats to the world's peace," Coop said.

"For how long?"

"As long as it takes, Kentu."

"I think it's time for a public discussion about the role of the US."

"We can talk after this crisis is over."

"It will be too late, Soldier," Kentu said.

"That 'Human Rights Commission' bullshit. Colonel Moammar Gadhafi bought a chair at the UN. We are lectured on moral rights by a rogue country responsible for murdering the passengers on Pan Am Flight 103 and those

Scottish people who were beneath the explosion."

Kentu shook his head. "Uncle Sam is the new Lex Luther."

"Huh?"

"Darth Vader, the Green Goblin. America never wanted peace. Heads its war. Tails its war. Why don't you make it more interesting? Get a two-headed coin. It's war. America has no eyes. No religion. No right to-"

"I'm not going to let some fourth-rate military power wipe me off the face of the earth."

"No one wanted this war. Join us, stop the war. War against terrorism. Terrorism is a concept. How the Hell are you ever going to fight a concept." Kentu said. "It's dragging us all into that cesspool of violence. That shit-slicked vat. That tidal wave. This is the fault of the right winged establishment. The electoral college is a fucking joke. Bush wasn't elected; he was selected. There's no way to peace. Peace is-"

Lucy called from upstairs. "Kentu, I thought you were going to the store."

"The shelves are empty, Ma." Kentu said yelling up to her.

"It's Code Orange, Kentu," Coop said to him.

"All that alert status business. It's worse than a snowstorm. No milk. No bread. I hope you're happy, solider."

"Kentu, I'm delirious with joy..."

"Go then. I thought your lack of sight would enable you to have some empathy, but you don't care. You don't see. This war is using our public schools' lunch money. These racists are taking away our scholarships."

"What does education and racism have to do with

war?" Coop asked.

"Exactly. Exactly."

"Blame America."

"You're damn right. What do you care about freedom?" Kentu asked.

"What do you care about freedom?" Coop asked.

"What do you care about freedom?" They both asked at the same time.

"Here we are steadily suffering from racism and classism. You would have been fine if you would have stayed out of this honkey oil imperialist right wing fundamentalist war. Well, I'm not taking it any more. All it takes is one raindrop to make an ocean. Thanks to people like you, we are in this collectivist nightmare. This quagmire. Each one of you who gets injured or killed helps. You got what you deserved."

"What?" Coop asked.

"You heard me."

"Say it again." Coop honed in on his voice.

"You heard me!" Kentu screamed.

"One more time."

"You got what you deserved."

Coop belted him. Kentu traveled back. Way back.

"I'd rather be alone in a hospital with my blind body and think about the world coming to an end that with you two fucking crazy people." Coop grabbed him and fought to hold his grip as Kentu attempted to twirl and pull away. "You asked me once if I knew what the enemy looked like. Well, I do. I know what the enemy looks like. It looks like confusion. And chaos. This is my country. Do you hear me? This land is my land. This land is your land. You are an American whether you like it or not. You can root for the enemy all you want but when it is said and done. If America falls, you fall. You motherfucking warmed over leftover freeze-dried hippies. Now put that in your peace pipe and smoke it."

Coop let go.

Kentu fell to the floor.

"Ask her about the voodoo doll?" Kentu asked as he got up.

"What the hell are you crapping on about, now?"

"Hoodoo is American voodoo, so I guess it would be a hoodoo doll."

"Don't tell me you believe in that?"

"Ask her."

"Ask who?" Coop asked.

"What other hero could I be talking about? For shit's sake, keep up."

Coop waved him away.

Kentu gave a nasty laugh and described candles everywhere. Hair like an explosion. A flowing black gown. He came home from the rally and saw it all.

"Why are you telling me this?"

"Because the séance was about you."

Kentu got the doll from under the sofa and gave it to Coop. "Feeling is believing."

Coop's fingers examined the doll in horror. He felt around it to find that the eyes had been drugged out.

"I don't know why she feels so attached to you. But you are different from the newspaperman and the mailman and the carpet cleaner man. It's not love, it's worse. I think you remind her of her father. It's the uniform."

"This is a voodoo doll?" Coop asked.

"Hoodoo. When you lose a parent that young, it ruins you sometimes."

"This country doesn't care. It keeps sending our fathers, our sons, our brothers over there and over there. The army doesn't care at all about families... She said it would bring you back to her. She didn't care what it took. A crash. An explosion. Hell, a slip and fall."

"She wished that I-"

"Just so that you'd come back. Think of it as friendly fire."

Coop dropped the doll. He heard her footsteps in his dark. Lucy entered. He felt around for the doll and hid it before she could see it.

Lucy eyed Coop. "Something wrong?"

"I'd like to speak to your mother alone."

"About what? Is something wrong?"

"Don't you have a rally to go to?" Coop asked Kentu.

"No, I have some shopping to do when I get back. Be sure and tell me if you need help packing your bags."

"What? Now why would I do that?" Lucy asked. She winked at Coop.

"He's under my care."

Kentu left.

"What's up?"

"What am I doing here?" Coop asked.

"What kind of question is that? You're recouping, Coop."

"You're bad for me, Lucy."

"No, I'm not. I only wish for the best for you."

"Do you believe in voodoo?"

"In America, it's called hoodoo."

"Do you believe in it?"

"Of course not. What do you think I'm crazy for?"

Coop threw the doll at her. "What do you call this?"

She caught it and said she called the doll 'Coop'.

"That's what I call it. It's my Coop doll."

"I'm getting out of here." He turned but tripped on some of her clutter.

"All right. So there's a doll. What's the big deal?"

"You wished for me to be struck blind?"

"Well, yes, or injured some other way." Lucy explained. "Go deaf in one ear during a firing. Lose an appendage. A foot maybe, or even up to the knee. Not the whole leg though."

"You're insane."

"Or that. Be certifiably crazy. They discharge you for that too. Anything so that you can come home to me." She took his arm to help him up.

"Don't touch me," he told her.

"You don't even know if it's permanent."

"I can't see a fucking thing."

"That's not so bad." She reached out for him.

"Said who? Don't touch me. You wished for me to be injured?"

"I can touch you; this is your home now. You're safe with me, Coop."

"Safe? Here?"

"I love you," she told him.

"Why did you have a voodoo doll?"

"I love you."

"Did you stick pins in it?"

"I mean well."

"Give me the phone," Coop demanded.

"It's not that I wished you ill. It's just the lesser of two evils."

Coop stammered around for the phone.

"Coop, I love you. I lit candles, and I prayed. Bring him to me. Whatever it takes. I don't even care about the rest of his unit."

"Well, I care about the rest of my unit."

"Bring him to me any way possible. Even if you have to injure him. Even if-"

"Do me and yourself a favor. Shut the Hell up."

He tripped over the clutter.

"I'll dial for you," she said.

"Get away from me. I would have gotten to it easier if this place wasn't such a mad house."

"All it's missing is a woman's touch. I'm a lady, remember?"

Coop clumsily dialed the phone.

"Hello. Hello. Is this the 250th Support Battalion, I'm Sergeant —" he stopped short. "This isn't the 250th? This is Pizza Paradise. No. No. Not even a deep dish."

Coop hung up.

"Let me dial. What's the number?"

"Go to Hell!" Coop screamed at her.

"I called the VA where I picked you up at."

"Hello. My name is Lucy. Lucia Baker. I was by the other day to pick up Sergeant Cooper of the 250th. Infantry. Yes. Yes."

Coop searched for the phone's receiver.

"Let me talk. You have to send someone over. I have to

get back there... No, it's not my eyes. No, I can't... I can't stay here any longer. Yes. Yes. That's the exact address. How soon can you be over?"

"How soon will they be over?"

Coop waved her away.

"Thank you. Thank you."

She leered. "How soon? I just want to know if there's enough time for us to-"

"You've got to be kidding."

"What do we have? An hour. I hope we have at least an hour before they come. All I want is one last time."

Coop pushed her away. Lucy started disrobing.

"Come on. Kentu isn't here. We have the place to ourselves. The night is still young. Come on."

An explosion shook the room. The lights went out. They were both hammered around.

"What happened? What?" Coop asked.

Coop could feel the darkness around him. His stomach froze up.

"All the power is off," Lucy screamed.

"Turn on the radio," Coop told her.

"The power is off."

"Don't you have any batteries?" Coop asked.

"No."

"I told you-"

"I didn't do it."

"Damn it. Turn it on anyway," he told her he heard her shifting about.

"But the power is off."

"Turn the radio on so that I'll know when the power comes back on. Do as I say!"

Lucy ran.

"And bring back a flashlight."

"I don't have one."

"Don't tell me that."

"It's the truth. Maybe the lights will come back on."

"Shut off the water and gas."

"How do you do that?" Lucy asked.

"Shit. Why? Why? Why? Did you not prepare? It's the right thing to do. You don't even have a fucking flashlight."

"This is not my fault."

"Where did you put my backpack?" Coop asked.

"I left it in the hospital."

"Shit."

"You don't need all that Army stuff here."

"Remember when I told you to get your stuff together. The emergency kit."

"Do you really think it was an explosion?" Lucy asked.

"The way the ground shook. Yes."

"I wonder what blew up."

"Take me over to the window."

Lucy led him to the window.

"What do you see?" Coop asked her.

"A whole lot of nothing," she reported. "The street is black."

"Shit."

"I wonder how long the lights are going to be out, Coop."

"I don't even hear any fire engine sirens."

"Neither do I."

"This is too weird. It's like being silent."

"The phone." Lucy ran to it.

"The phone is dead."

"Look, the nearest emergency shelter is Krewstown Road. If this goes on-"

"Let's wait till my son gets back."

"Your son?" Coop asked.

"The market is just up the block."

"I know where it is."

"Kentu will be here."

"So will the MPs."

"They'll come. They'll come for us."

Coop paused to let her words sink in. "It's still and silent."

"I have a book of matches."

"Get it."

Lucy left the room and Coop felt the tether stretch. He thought if only he'd become an astronaut, right then he could be in orbit with a hose carrying oxygen.

Someone tried the door.

"Lucy?" Coop asked.

"I'm looking," he said.

He could hear her shifting about as the door burst open.

"Lucy is someone at the door."

"What?" Lucy asked.

"The-" Coop began but couldn't go on. He smelled the stench and heard a huff then what sounded like a snort.

He next heard one single breathe, followed by agitated breathing. Someone or something was lurking.

"Lucy?" Coop asked as he advanced toward the door.

"What?" Lucy asked from the other room.

"Shhhhh." Coop told her.

The door busted open. Two ski-masked men stood

upright in the doorway and flashed a flood light on Coop.

"Oh, this is too good," one man said, his blue, round eyes shining.

"Identify yourself," Coop said.

"Just take it easy. This won't take long," the man said.

The intruder opened up his satchel and started going through the drawers.

"What are you doing? Stop," Coop said.

"I'll be through in a minute. Take it easy," the intruder said.

Coop stumbled across the room. The intruder averted his grip. Coop knew that voice. Speed up the first time he heard it. Slowed down the time before this. This time it was hyped up and loaded but in the middle of the road.

"I found the matches," Lucy said, coming back into the room.

"Well, well, this just gets better and better," the first guy said.

The masked man up and downed her.

"I don't have any valuables," Lucy told him.

"I'm sure you have something that I want," the intruder said.

"Get away from her," Coop told him.

The intruder laughed. He stepped closer.

"Don't move," Coop said.

The intruder with the dark eyes advanced towards as he took off his belt.

"Run," Coop yelled.

Lucy was frozen with fright.

"Why don't you stay out of this?" the intruder asked him.

109

The intruder began to undo his pants.

"Lucy, run. Go back upstairs. Lock the door."

"No, stay right there. This won't take long," the first intruder said.

"Hey, you don't have to do this. This is a dump. They don't have anything here," the other man said.

"Johns?" Coop asked.

"Coop?" Johns asked.

"What are you doing breaking into people's houses?" Coop asked.

"Why is your face all wrapped up?" Johns asked.

"Who's gonna help you, this blind guy?" he asked Lucy.

The intruder made a run toward her.

Coop tackled him and beat at him blindly. The intruder gasped and kicked as Coop bumped his head against the wall. Together, they jerked and whirled. Coop gripped him and sent him sprawling. Coop felt for him to try and pin him before he rose.

The intruder wiggled away. He grabbed Lucy.

"I've got her now."

Lucy screamed.

"Is that your man or your son?" the intruder asked.

"Let her go!" Johns yelled.

"Shut up," the intruder told him.

"Let her go," Coop made another grab for him.

"Stay out of it," The intruder told him.

"Get out of here," Coop told him.

"I told you to shut up," the intruder told him.

Coop said his name. "Johns."

"Coop. Is that you under all those bandages?"

"You know him."

"Why are you doing this, Johns?" Coop asked.

"I got caught up," Johns said.

"You took an oath," Coop said.

"Oh, come on," Johns said.

"I don't get this," Lucy said.

"You want the whole puzzle put together, but the pieces will never fit," Johns said. "When you last left me, Coop, I was a murderer, don't act like this is such a surprise."

"When I last saw you were a piano player," Coop said.

"I've got a baby on the way," Johns said.

A gust of air blew in the room.

"Oh, shit," Johns said.

Kentu pulled out this gun and fired at the intruder but struck his mother.

"Ma!" Kentu screamed.

"Lucy!" Coop screamed.

"Oh!" Johns said and took off running.

The other man ran too.

Kentu took after the intruder with his gun.

Coop felt his way over too. He noticed that her hand was limp. Her flesh was already icy. He stroked her hair for a moment then Coop fell on the floor and found the intruder's knife.

Coop held his weapon tightly.

He eased himself against the wall then over to the corner. Darkness swallowed him whole. Next in this crazy house with a dead woman, he wondered what enemy would barge his face when it was hot, under his bandages sweat trickled down the sides of his nose.

As the moments came and passed, he steeled himself against fear. He told himself that he wasn't helpless. He vowed to fight against being captured. He promised himself he would make it. The lights went on. The music from the radio came on. The light and music went off.

This happened four times while he was huddled in the corner. Then the lights went out for a sustained period.

He murmured, "The-the-the Lord is my shepherd. I sh-sh-shall not want to. He maketh me-"

The light came back on. The music blared.

Twenty-Two

Coop lay in a VA hospital bed. The doctor in a white lab coat was by his side.

"I thought that in a VA hospital the doctors were never around. Don't you guys usually call us by the wrong name, and mix up charts," Coop said.

"This isn't going to be like 'Nam where the vet gets the shaft. Disrespected and neglected. You must have watched too many bad movies..." Doc said.

"I'm surprised you still came out to get me."

"Leave no man behind."

"Doc, what blew up?"

"Coop, you're getting yourself all worked up again."

"But Doc-"

"Don't overexert yourself, Coop, please. There's nothing you or I can do about it now."

"You're not going to tell me what happened?"

"Coop, that's not your concern, your bandages are ready to come off."

Doc helped Coop into a wheelchair. "Let's hope that you've healed. Hopefully, this will be a brand-new day for you. Your first day without the military. If your vision is restored, even the VA hospital will be behind you. The rest of your life is ahead of you…Looks like the makings of a beautiful spring day."

Down with America.

Doc shook his head. "Hippies and draft card burners."

"What does it all mean? What is it all for? In my head, I hear the speakers and the cheering and the shouting. Who's right, Doc. Who's right? I mean this is an incredibly asinine question. But please, I must understand. Some people are against the war. I hear them in my head."

"You hear voices in your head?"

"They're saying 'Down with America'".

"That's not in your head. Those are those confounded protesters.

He shouted out the window. "Hey, people are trying to convalesce here."

"I don't remember the blast that blinded me."

"Maybe you're not blind, Coop. The bandages come off today."

"I don't think I loved her, Doc."

"That woman who you were staying with?"

"I do miss her."

"There're some women that you love and other women that you miss."

"The whole thing is so crazy, Doc."

"That's the problem with the world; there is too much craziness. Pretty soon someday there will be so much craziness that we won't be able to contain or treat. There will be too many to lock away. Rational thought is getting rarer and rarer."

Down with America.

"This is a hospital. We are trying to make sick people well," Doc shouted.

"They remind me of those anti-abortion people who

kill people to stop abortions. Or those people who hang out outside a death row court case."

"You know who gets good health care, Doc, people on death row. They give you top of the line medical care. They make sure you are completely healthy for the state to execute."

"Some states even ask you how you'd like to die."

"I'd say: old age," Coop said.

SUCK MY DICK.

"Quiet!" Doc yelled back at them.

"How about that last meal business?" Coop asked. "Only to crap it out moments later after that sodium pentathlon started coursing through your veins," Coop said.

"Praying for a call from the governor."

"Why don't they call the governor, Doc?"

"Maybe they don't have a cell phone…" Doc laughed at his turn of phrase. "Let's take those bandages off."

"Don't I get my news? Are you going to tell me what happened?"

"Don't worry yourself about the news." The doctor told him as he went to the open window and took a deep breath. "It looks like the makings of a beautiful spring day." Doc left the room.

"Doc, Doc," Coop called.

Doc rushed back into the room. His eyebrows crazed and arched. "I'm sorry I didn't realize you were still talking. What were you saying?" Doc asked.

"I'm not afraid."

"Well, good, that's good Sergeant Cooper. Coop. What's that quote? There is nothing to fear-"

Coop finished it. "But fear itself."

"I can't go back, and I can't go forward. I don't know what the future is going to be. Doc, could you read me the paper?"

"You may be able to read it yourself in a few moments."

No war. No war.

"Surrender is near," Doc said.

"Whose?" Coop asked.

DOWN WITH AMERICA.

"I know things look bad, Coop, health and mental health resources in affected communities are overwhelmed. Across the country, there's a significant number of casualties."

"It's a little hot in here. Could you open a window?" Coop asked.

"I already opened it." The doctor told him. They wheeled him over to the window.

"Any plans of what you want to do?" Doc asked.

"Twenty."

"Twenty?"

"Twenty. Then I retire. Maybe 25 to sweeten the pot."

"We'll take care of you. Good care. There're plenty of programs."

"Programs?" Coop asked. "I'm 27."

"That is a great age."

"But what will I do? Without the army and being blind."

"Blind civilians lead productive lives. Do you like to read? There's Braille."

"I'm 27," Coop said.

"That's a great age. What I wouldn't give—I'd give my right arm… I wouldn't worry about any of this."

He reached for the bandages.

DOWN WITH AMERICA.

"Wait a minute. Wait," Coop halted Doc's hands. "Law and order upside down. All this turmoil and conflict. No sign of relief in the near future."

Doc reassured," But you're safe here… You couldn't be safer. You're safe here."

Off in the distance, the protesters chanted.

"They're out there, gathered with their signs and their slogans."

"They'll get tired after a while and things will get back to normal," Doc said wearily.

"Normal?" I asked. Four hands steadied me as I rose to my feet. "Normal with the widows and the orphans? The bombed-out buildings? With billions of dollars spent, Doc. Doctor?"

"Please-"

"You call this normal?"

"There's something that's been pushing to the back of my head. "

"Yes, yes we're listening."

"There was a woman with a meat cleaver."

"However, this shakes out, after the last bomb is dropped, after the last shot is fired, after the last protest sign is lowered, what is going to be there to greet us? Are things going to get better?"

That's what's wrong with the world. People forget that others have to live. Health and mental health resources in affected communities are overwhelmed."

"But I was like that. I've been in so long already. I wasn't used to questioning anything."

"Son, the bandages."

Just then the door swung open. A woman entered. Tall. Lithe. Half clothed in red torn fishnets, black high boots, and thigh lengthened hot pink peacoat.

"Coop, I'm so glad I found you," she gushed. "You don't know what I've been through to get here. The check points. The pat downs. The cavity searches. It was like I never left work."

"Good God! Who are you?" the doctor asked.

"Marilyn?" Coop asked.

"You know this woman?" the doctor asked.

"What have they done to you?" Marilyn said she rushed toward him.

"Don't touch him," the doctor warned and separated her from him. "He's just about to be compromised. The bandages are just about to come off."

Marilyn stood back.

A few moments passed.

Doc gave a reassuring, confident smile as he took off the bandages. "What do you see?"

Coop stood up, blinked, and walked about the room without feeling his way. Disembodied, foreign to him, these steps, his legs were. In the harsh early light, his eyes were flooded not with images but ideas. And though he could see, darkness spread over him anew like a black, heavy familiar blanket.

Coop eyed the doctor who was a brother just as he had guessed. He was a solidly built man of about 55 with silver flecked hair and skin like a seal. Coop peered at his bed about the room then he gazed out the window.

He thought of her. The way she appeared. She was pretty though he didn't think so at first sight. In that filthy house that she hadn't cleaned in decades, she was a contrast. She always looked and smelled like she just took a bath. He considered all the mothers he met on his mission –the plump, the visibly old, the sane. The shriveled, wizened, toothless. Those that he held as they wept and worried about the future of their sons. And that one lady, what was her name who held herself with such dignity.

Coop thought of that first time they had sex and that unjustified bliss that filled his lungs.

The chanting subsides.

Saved for the pitiless darkness for this,

He focused back on Doc. Then on his sister. Then back to the doctor.

He walked over to the window. For a moment, a blue milky flash danced before him.

Down with America?

In the 20-degree weather, they were down there in their thin jackets, trudging across the lawn, fists raised high. Coop felt like he was drowning against these rancid waters. He turned to go back to the room. Coop held its inhabitants in his deliberate, unwavering gaze.

"Coop, hey…" Marilyn said, her voice has a quaver as she readjusted her bra strap.

Doc's mouth was slightly agape, now unsure. He held Coop's glasses. "What do you see, Coop?"

"Nothing."

THE END

About the Author

Allison Whittenberg won the John Steinbeck Writing Award, Judith Siegel Pearson Award, and several Pushcart Prize nominations. Her novels include *Sweet Thang*, *Hollywood and Maine*, *Life is Fine*, *Tutored through Random House*. Her collection of short stories *Carnival of Reality* was published by Apprentice Press in 2022. She currently teaches creative writing in Drexel University's MFA program.

Apprentice House is the country's only campus-based, student-staffed book publishing company. Directed by professors and industry professionals, it is a nonprofit activity of the Communication Department at Loyola University Maryland.

Using state-of-the-art technology and an experiential learning model of education, Apprentice House publishes books in untraditional ways. This dual responsibility as publishers and educators creates an unprecedented collaborative environment among faculty and students, while teaching tomorrow's editors, designers, and marketers.

Eclectic and provocative, Apprentice House titles intend to entertain as well as spark dialogue on a variety of topics. Financial contributions to sustain the press's work are welcomed. Contributions are tax deductible to the fullest extent allowed by the IRS.

To learn more about Apprentice House books or to obtain submission guidelines, please visit www.apprenticehouse.com.

Apprentice House
Communication Department
Loyola University Maryland
4501 N. Charles Street
Baltimore, MD 21210
Ph: 410-617-5265
info@apprenticehouse.com • www.apprenticehouse.com

Ingram Content Group UK Ltd.
Milton Keynes UK
UKHW050716090623
422929UK00045B/557